Wolf Claw

JES DREW

Covert art by Stefanidi Marina

Copyright © 2016 Jes Drew
All rights reserved.
ISBN: 1540519945
ISBN-13: 978-1540519948

Because I could not stop for Death –
He kindly stopped for me –
The Carriage held but just Ourselves –
And Immortality.

We slowly drove – He knew no haste
And I had put away
My labor and my leisure too,
For His Civility –

We passed the School, where Children strove
At Recess – in the Ring –
We passed the Fields of Gazing Grain –
We passed the Setting Sun –

Or rather – He passed Us –
The Dews drew quivering and Chill –
For only Gossamer, my Gown –
My Tippet – only Tulle –

We paused before a House that seemed
A Swelling of the Ground –
The Roof was scarcely visible –
The Cornice – in the Ground –

Since then – 'tis Centuries – and yet
Feels shorter than the Day
I first surmised the Horses' Heads
Were toward Eternity –
-Emily Dickinson

Dedication:

To story lovers everywhere. Also, to Jesus,
Who has written *my* story with love.

Prologue

When I was seven years old, I was scarred for life- literally.

"Is Mommy coming home today?" I asked.

Father looked up from his desk. Around us was our home library; an impressive collection of every faerie story and legend on paper since the dawn of time to that fateful year, 1916- or at least so it seemed to my seven-year-old mind. "I'm sorry, Janie," he said. "But no. She's a very busy woman, you know."

I frowned. Mommy had gone off to work at her mysterious job once I turned four, and though she visited often, she never seemed to be around.

Now she's never around.

Anyway, still being a child, I quickly forgot the cause of my frown and ran off to find something to amuse myself. What I found was my big brother, Peter Thomas, who was nine at the time (the last year he went by his full name).

"Do you want to come outside and play with me?" I asked eagerly, already knowing what the answer would be. We were each others' only playmates, after all.

"Sure," he had answered, blowing the auburn- the color we both shared- hair out of his eyes. "Just got to feed the dogs first."

I nodded eagerly before running out the door.

Our home lies in a small clearing in the middle of a large forest, without so much as a road to connect us to society. At the time, I didn't even know there *was* such a thing as society. I was content simply to explore the part of the woods adjacent to our clearing, looking for flowers to make a bouquet for Mommy- for whenever she returned. Indeed, that's what I found myself doing that particular evening.

My eyes fell on a flower, its color a cross between purple and silver- the exact same shade of my eyes (and Mommy's and Thomas'). Intrigued, I leaned over and picked it, fingering its petals.

Then I heard a growl.

I looked up and found a massive wolf standing on its hind legs, towering over me. Its fur was black as midnight, and its eerily human eyes locked on mine. I attempted to scream, but my voice deserted me. As did my feet, which sent me toppling backwards.

The wolf dropped down on all fours and then stretched one claw toward me, one nail slashing the skin just to the left of my left eye.

"Get away from her!" Thomas screamed somewhere behind me, and the wolf seemed to smile. Then it obeyed Thomas and ran off with surprising speed.

Stunned, I reached up to feel my face, and felt the warmth of blood. Distantly, I felt a sting, but I was more concerned with the strange, hazy images dancing before my eyes.

Thomas reached my side and asked a million questions at once, but I couldn't focus. Instead, I lifted my small hand and studied it through my hallucinations:

the forest moving around me, the sounds of distant howling, and eyes both wolfish and human watching my every move. Strangest of all, though, were the hallucinations surrounding my own hand.

"Wolf claw," I whispered.

Chapter One

In which I sit at my father's bedside, dream of society, and bid farewell to my brother

Almost ten years after my strange encounter with the wolf, I find myself at Father's bedside.

"Why did you do this to yourself, Father?" I ask. "You've been in your library day and night. Now you've gone and broken your health. Why?" He's always been a workaholic, spending every spare moment in his library, but he'd become worse these recent weeks, not sparing a moment for life outside the library as he pored over his many volumes with an almost desperate passion.

Father, his eyes as feverish as his obsession with his books, reaches up and pushes aside the bangs I've grown long for the purpose of concealing the scar the wolf gave me. Then he runs his finger down it.

I close my eyes, trying to block out the strange images that come to my mind whenever I or someone touches the scar: teeth, claws, anger…

"I won't let it take you," Father mutters. "I won't."

"You're not making any sense, Father."

"Bring me my books."

"No, Father- you must *rest*."

"Then bring me my Thomas."

I study my father. It's not only his eyes that are sick, but everything: his auburn hair Thomas and I inherited is damp with sweat, his face much paler than usual, and his hands are shaking ever so slightly. Pursing my lips, I go to fetch my brother.

I find him outside, chopping firewood, his favorite

chore now that I'm in charge of taking care of the dogs (for some reason they only answer to me now).

"Father needs you," I tell him.

Thomas, nineteen now and both tall and strong- much more capable should the wolf show its ugly face around here again- immediately puts down his ax and rushes inside, but I stay out in the crisp autumn air. To think, my seventeenth birthday will soon be upon me. Likely, not much will happen in the way of celebration. Mother, who I would assume to be dead by now if it weren't for her frequent letters, probably won't visit, which she hasn't done since the wolf attacked. However, Father promised he'd take me to a city and introduce me to society- something I've longed to do for most of my reclusive life (once I realized that there *was* a society, that is). I've only been to the city once, and that brief visit ended in disaster, but it still hasn't lost its allure.

Now, though, I just hope that Father will survive. I can't lose him- he and Thomas are all I really have. I can't lose *either* of them.

I shudder as the wind whips my unfashionably long hair against my face.

If I lose Father, it would be the wolf's fault. Father, being a historian of legends, saw more in the wolf attack than most others would. Since the wolf, Father, who was always diligent in his studies, has become almost desperate- especially recently, which is odd since it has been almost a whole decade since the attack. But I suppose the lines between fantasy and reality have become blurred for him.

Then again, what is reality?

I shudder again. If only I could figure out the truth of the matter; then I might be able to fix the problems that have beset my home since the wolf scarred me. Then I might be able to banish the strange images that have haunted me since I received the scar, those images when it was almost like I was seeing out of a wolf's eyes...

"Jane!" Thomas calls.

I turn around and face my brother. His expression is uncharacteristically somber and... scared? "What is it, Tom?"

"I'm leaving."

"Leaving! But why? Father is ill- "

"That is why I must go. If Father hadn't fallen ill, he'd be the one going, but that isn't the case now. Look, I plan on returning in time for your birthday. But if I don't-"

"No, you can't leave; I need your help. *Father* needs your help."

"And this is my helping him- and you."

"Stop speaking in riddles and just tell me what's going on, Thomas."

He shakes his head. "Life *is* a riddle. Now, Jane, listen to me-"

"But you're not listening to *me-*"

Thomas grabs me by my shoulders and looks me in the eyes with a more intense gaze than I've ever seen on him. "If I don't return in time for your birthday, you are to take yourself and Father and go into the cellar. Seal the doors and don't leave until you absolutely have to- and whatever you do, *do not* leave at night."

I blink and nod slowly. "All right."

He sighs in relief and releases me. "Take care, sister."

"You too, brother. But where are you going? Won't you at least tell me that?"

He pats the rifle at his side- the one Father had specifically made to shoot silver bullets (Father has read entirely too many books about monsters that can only be stopped with silver bullets). "I'm going hunting."

Chapter Two

In which I face a moral dilemma, meet a friend of my mother's, and have nightmares while I am still awake

Suddenly, I see my brother tracking wolf prints. A bead of sweat rolls down his face, and I can tell that he's scared. This scares me somewhat; my brother does not scare easily. He looks around and I get the feeling that he feels like he's being watched.

Worst of all, I see this scene out of the eyes of a wolf.

I sit up in my bed and find myself sweating as much as my brother had been in my dream.

Thomas is in trouble. He needs help, but how can I give it when our father needs me here?

I climb out of bed and go to check on Father, trying to ignore the dream. Trying to ignore the fact that I know it was- *somehow*- far more than just a dream.

Five years ago, my father's old college roommate, Vincent Drumlins, rented our extra room. Father had Thomas and me call him 'Uncle Vincent' even though neither of us saw him as an uncle; Uncle Vincent was grouchy and even more reclusive than we are. Besides that, there was something *off* about him- something creepy. We used to joke that he was a vampire. Anyway, two years ago, when the moon was full, Uncle Vincent went out to have some 'quiet time.' That night, I dreamed I glimpsed him attacked by something with wolf claws. And I saw it through the eyes of Uncle Vincent's attacker.

The next morning, I had assumed it was just a dream, but then Uncle Vincent never came home. I can't let whatever happened to Uncle Vincent happen to Thomas.

"Jane?" Father calls as I enter his room.

"I'm here," I assure, hurrying to his side.

Father smiles and closes his eyes.

However, I frown. Both Thomas and Father need me, but I can help only one. Though, how I could help Thomas, I don't know. Still, I feel that if I were with him, there might be *something* I could do...

Oh, what is the honorable thing to do?

Shaking my head, I go to the kitchen and begin making some soup for Father. I'm frequently interrupted, though, since Father keeps trying to get out of bed. By the time I finish his breakfast, we're both drained, and I have to spoon feed him.

"What am I going to do with you?" I ask.

"What am I going to do with you?" Father echoes before drifting off to sleep.

"What am I going to do with you *and* Thomas?" I whisper, straightening up.

I do all that I can do for now: soak a rag for Father's forehead and wash his soup bowl. Then I'm left with nothing, but a horrible gnawing feeling that Thomas is in trouble and there is absolutely nothing I can do for *him*.

"It's probably nothing," I try to tell myself. "I mustn't be so pessimistic."

When my next thought is of Uncle Vincent, I decide to go outside.

Today is cooler than yesterday, with more of a bite. Ignoring the shivers going down my spine, I decide to go pick flowers to cheer up Father- and myself. I haven't picked flowers since the wolf incident, always scared history would repeat itself (I've heard Father mention repetitions in both legends and history far too often), but if there is a wolf out there, it would be better if it came after me rather than after Thomas. Though it would be best if it didn't come after anyone at all...

I shake my head and focus on my current objective. Years though it may have been, I still remember the best place to find a good assortment of flowers; the very same place the wolf scratched me, in fact. I go there first.

It's smaller than I remember, but otherwise exactly the same. Kneeling down, I begin to pick, keeping my ears alert in case Father awakes, or Thomas returns. Or the wolf.

Thankfully, nothing happens, and I'm able to gather a large bouquet. Straightening up, I notice something I hadn't before: a line of even incisions on my old favorite climbing tree.

Curious, I approach it and find that the incisions appear to be nine tally marks. Possibly Thomas put them there to keep track of how many feet he managed to climb on the tree. Strange thing is, they look like they were done at different times.

And why does seeing those marks make my scar feel like it's on fire?

Looking away, I begin to see strange images not unlike the hallucinations that have haunted me since childhood.

Thomas lies against a tree, napping, with his rifle resting in his lap. He no doubt thinks he's prepared to fire it at a moment's notice. Little does he know that the moment's notice has already passed and he is being watched, not just by me but also the person whose eyes I am seeing through. Someone with large hands and long, dirty nails. Hands that I somehow know belong to a killer.

Jerking awake like Thomas needs to, I flee to my cottage, losing several flowers on the way. Once inside, I slam the back door shut, and try to calm my racing heart.

But how can I calm it? There is something evil in these woods with us, and Thomas is out there all alone... No, not alone, and that's the worst part.

I glance over to my still-sleeping father. He needs me, but Thomas may very well need me more. I have to go find him, warn him- and see for myself what this creature is before I go utterly insane, if I'm not already.

Knock. Knock. Knock.

The dogs, Romulus and Remus, both start barking and my heart goes racing all over again. Dropping the bouquet, I pick up the nearest weapon (we have them all over the house), Thomas' hatchet, and go to the door. When I open it, I find a rather ugly girl about my age wearing a nurse's uniform.

I lower the hatchet and signal for the dogs to calm down, and they obey immediately, lowering their ears and bringing their tails between their legs. Then I turn back to the stranger. "Who are you and what are you doing here?"

"I'm Priscilla," she answers happily. "Your mother sent me to nurse your father. She said that after I do she'll give me three wishes!"

"My... my mother?"

Priscilla nods and hands me a piece of paper with my mother's business stamp on top of it- the same stamp she uses on every letter she sends us.

So, this girl really is from Mother then. I'm not sure what she means about Mother granting her three wishes, but I've never completely understood the business that keeps Mother away from us. I do, however, know that even if she has left us, she means us no harm. This girl is just what I need. "Thank you... Priscilla? Uh, how is my mother?"

"Oh, she's doing very well; just glowing." Priscilla giggles at some inside joke.

I nod slowly. "Uh-huh. What was that you said about three wishes?"

"Well, you know, sometimes deserving girls who have tragic pasts get lucky and meet your mother like I did."

"Actually, I *don't* know." Am I not deserving enough to have my own mother? Or is she just trying to help me with getting my own tragic past?

"Well, it's pretty simple. Since I've been teased my whole life, your mothers says I meet the tragic part but to get my wishes I have to fulfill the deserving part. So here I am." She smiles like that explains everything.

I stare at her long and hard before shaking my head. Since I can't seem to get anything reasonable out of her, I just let Priscilla in and lead her to Father's bedside.

The girl scans him before giggling. "It's just exhaustion. He should be better in no time. Then I'll get my three wishes!" She giggles again.

Maybe she's *not* what I need... But she'll have to do. "Listen to me very carefully, Priscilla. I have to go out looking for my brother. I don't know how long I'll be gone, but if I'm not back before twenty-two days have passed, take my father and seal yourselves up in the cellar for as long as you can, and whatever you do, *don't leave at night.*"

Priscilla smiles and nods like I have just told her the most wonderful thing.

Wow, she's not even asking questions. I wouldn't be able to survive without asking questions. "Well, I have to pack up," I say, leaving Priscilla with my father. I hope I'm doing the right thing.

I dress in layers of my brother's hand-me-downs- the only kinds of clothes I've ever really worn since Mother left, taking her feminine touch with her (no doubt to reward it to *deserving* girls)- and boots (also hand-me-downs). Then I pack a few more changes of clothing into a backpack with some food, water, rope, a compass, a flashlight, and a dagger. Father trained Thomas and me to use about every weapon from a bow to a pistol, and everything in between, but the dagger is my preferred weapon. It reminds me of claws...

"I'm leaving now!" I call as I pull my hair into a ponytail.

"Have fun!" Priscilla calls before giggling.

I roll my eyes and go to Father's side. "Good-bye."

Father is too deep asleep to respond.

Pressing my lips to his forehead, I turn to leave.

When I step out of the cottage I've spent my entire life in except for the day my Father tried to move us to the city when I was eight, I shudder. After all, the one night we spent in the city was plagued by a freak wolf attack that convinced my father that the city was as bad as our cottage, only with extra dangers.

I shoulder my backpack and a rifle, pick up Thomas' hatchet again, and step into the woods. Though I know these woods well, they've always seemed like a magical world. A magical world rife with dangers.

Obviously, I've read too many of Father's books.

Analyzing the forest, I find a sign of my brother- a snapped branch at his height- and become immersed in following his trail.

Then I hear a twig snap to my left.

My heart proves that it is a creature of habit and begins racing again, and I break into a cold sweat. Then, very slowly, I raise my head to see whatever it is that has approached me without my noticing it until now.

What I find is an animal larger than I have ever seen before, and whiter than I even realized an animal could be. Pure and majestic, I find myself gazing upon a – the? -white stag.

I look at it and it looks at me. What goes through its mind, I do not know. As for my mind, I think of all the contradicting legends around the white stag. Some say it is a harbinger of good luck, while others believe it is an ill omen. Still others argue that it can be either, depending on how you treat it and how it reacts to you. Even those legends disagree- is it noble or evil to kill the stag? Or does it matter only whether or not your arrow hits true? Is the stag itself noble or evil? Does it guide lost maidens to safety or deeper into the forest to die? Are humans noble or evil, and does that even have any relevance to the legend of the stag?

Because I know the answer to whether people are noble or evil, I back away a step. But the stag obviously doesn't share my knowledge, because he steps closer.

Its large, star-like eyes lock on mine and I forget all the legends that surround it and reach out my hand. The stag doesn't move and my hand touches its soft nose.

"You're beautiful," I whisper.

The stag makes no noise, but seems to be saying something with its soulful eyes. A warning.

"What is it?" I ask. "Is something trying to hurt you? Hurt me?"

The stag bobs its head as if to say yes.

"Who? What?"

A twig snaps behind me and I turn. This time it's only a bird. When I turn back around, though, the stag is gone.

I blink. Was it ever there?

Shivering, I wrap my arms around myself. It's gotten colder. And darker.

Night has fallen.

I turn my flashlight on and continue searching.

Gasp.

I pause, my head beginning to hurt. Then it happens again: my hallucinations make me see through another's eyes.

"I will kill you," Thomas says.

The one whose eyes I see through snarls. "Not if I kill you first."

"No," I whisper, leaning against a tree. "Please, no."

Thomas aims his gun and pulls the trigger.

Suddenly, my arm hurts and I fall to my knees.

The one whose life I am viewing lunges at Thomas.

"No!" I scream, and then everything goes black.

Chapter Three

In which I meet a handsome stranger, help hunt a werewolf, and learn some very, very bad news.

"Miss?" someone calls. "Miss, are you all right?"

I open my eyes and find myself lying on the forest floor. Then I roll over and find myself looking up at a boy about Thomas' age, but who is most definitely *not* Thomas. This boy is slightly taller and leaner than my robust brother, and instead of auburn hair and blue eyes, this boy has dirty blonde hair and green eyes. Also, while my brother (and consequently I) wear mostly plaid shirts and thick trousers, this boy wears a simple light green outfit and a strange knitted hat.

My jaw drops. Besides Father, Thomas, and Uncle Vincent- and none of them count anyway- this is the first boy I've ever seen. And he is *some* specimen.

So, this is what *it* is.

"Miss?"

I remember myself (good looking or not, he is a potential threat- probably more so *because* of his good looks), grab my hatchet, and aim it at the boy. "What do you want?"

He puts his hands in the air. "I don't mean you any harm, Miss, but you seemed like you needed help."

Good enough for me. I put my hatchet down and sit up. "I'm searching for my brother. Have you seen him? He looks a rather lot like me, only slightly taller- I think I might catch up to him, but he doesn't agree- and with shorter hair- much, much shorter, though still kind of shaggy. Have you seen him?"

"I'm afraid not." The boy offers me his hand.

I take it and he effortlessly pulls me up and I try to control my heart at its frantic panic over the touch.

"I'm Amos Hood, by the way," he adds, removing his strange hat.

"Jane Delane." My eyes fall on the strangely shaped leather on his back with a hilt protruding from it. A sword in a sheath? "What are you doing here?"

"Hunting."

Of course; it seems to be hunting season around here. "Hunting for what?" Could he and Thomas be hunting for the same thing?

Or maybe for each other.

I back away slightly.

"Doesn't matter," Amos answers. "Do you live near here?"

"Possibly."

"I must escort you home then. These woods aren't safe right now, *especially* at night."

"I have to find my brother."

"I'll look for him, but you need to go home before dark."

I narrow my eyes. "What are you hunting exactly? It *does* matter."

He shakes his head. "You wouldn't believe me."

"Try me." I cross my arms and plant my feet to show him I'm not going anywhere until he tells me what's going on.

Amos studies me for a long moment before answering. "A werewolf."

I purse my lips expecting to find myself skeptical only

to be surprised at how easily I accept his words. After all, why wouldn't it be a werewolf? Still... "Have you actually seen it?"

He nods. "I have. You probably don't believe me, but it is my duty to hunt creatures like werewolves and vampires."

"I think I do believe you. My father studies legends and I've always wondered... What do you know about this wolf?"

Amos replaces his hat, his eyes never leaving my face like he's trying to understand me. "I've been tracking it since I came across it in Chicago."

"Chicago? This is Ohio. Do you have any idea why it might have wandered all the way here?"

"I'm not sure, but it appears to be on the hunt- though for who or what, I do not know." Amos continues to study me for a long moment before asking, "Was there anything particularly unusual about your brother's disappearance?"

I run my hand through my hair nervously, not wanting to understand what he's hinting at. "Well, he left two days ago to go hunting. He... he took a rifle that can shoot silver bullets."

Amos groans. "It must be hunting your brother then, and he knew it..."

"No," I whisper. "No, no, no, no, no!"

"I have to get you home now," Amos says. "Then I must find your brother before it's too late- if it isn't already."

The air rushes from my lungs. "Too late?"

"Dead or turned."

Hope glimmers in my chest. "Then there's another option besides death?"

Amos frowns. "To be turned is a fate worse than death."

A chill runs down my spine. What could be worse than death? "But there *is* a cure for this turning, right?"

He shakes his head slowly. "None that I am aware of. Well, besides..." He reaches back and twists his sword in its sheath absently.

Another chill runs down my spine. Would this Amos kill Thomas if he is turned? "Take me with you." I don't care if Thomas is turned or not, I will *not* let him be killed- by a wolf or by Amos.

"Now, Miss- "

"Jane. My name is Jane."

"Jane, then. I don't believe that would be the wisest course of action."

"It is," I counter. "And I can give you four good reasons. First, this is my brother; I know him better than you- better than anyone, for that matter. Second, I know these woods better than you- and everyone else except maybe Thomas, really. Third, I am familiar with legends and will be a very valuable asset. Fourth, my mind is a valuable tool that would be foolish to cast aside." Father is always saying that I'm a genius; that I think on a different plane than normal people.

And then there are the images...

Amos smiles wryly. "Those four 'good reasons' all rest on your own assumptions that you have special knowledge of something- and none of it can actually be proven at the moment."

"I could prove to you that I'm an expert on Lycanthropy," I counter. "But somehow, I think it'll just be easier for you to know that if you do not let me come with you, I'll just go on my own, and I won't be returning home until I've found my brother- no matter how many days and *nights* it takes me."

Amos clenches his jaw. "You are a very stubborn young lady, Miss."

"I am aware of that. And it's Jane."

He narrows his eyes at me before turning around and starting to walk away.

I watch him. Is he leaving me?

He looks over his shoulder. "Don't lag behind, Miss. We have a werewolf to hunt and a brother to find. Hopefully those two things won't be one and the same."

~~~

My eyes constantly dance around our surroundings, expecting to see either Thomas or a wolf jump out of the woods. To keep my mind off of such dark things that are just *asking* for my hallucinations to begin again, I ask, "So, where are *you* from, Amos?"

Amos looks back at me, looking rather confused by my sudden question.

"I mean, I know the wolf is from Chicago, but what about you?"

"The wolf isn't from Chicago. That's only where I came across its path."

"Oh, so *you're* from Chicago then."

He shakes his head. "No, my family actually lives not

far from here."

"Then why were you in Chicago?"

Amos glances back at me, looking like he can't decide whether to be annoyed or not. "My duty takes me all over the country. I happened to be in Chicago because I had heard rumors that certain men who fit the description of vampires had joined Al Capone's gang. Then I followed a strange trail of unnatural clues to an abandoned building with signs that an itinerant wolf had passed through. Since it was obviously on the hunt for something, and therefore in its most dangerous state, I took up to my own hunt for it. Its trail led me here. I was half afraid it was after-" He looks back at me and stops himself. "A girl I know."

I can't help but smile mischievously. "Oh, a *girl* you know."

"Not like that."

"Then why are you being so secretive?"

"For her own safety."

I frown and close my mouth. We spend the rest of the day in silence.

Amos proves to be just as skilled at tracking as I am- maybe even more so, though I'd never admit that out loud. Together, we follow Thomas's trail to an area that has obviously seen a fight.

On the ground lies the smashed remains of the rifle that shoots- *shot*- silver bullets.

"No," I whisper, picking up the pieces, looking, *hoping* for some sign that my brother is still alive.

Thomas can't be dead. He's always been so alive, so obviously- using inductive reasoning that is- he's still alive now. He can't just be dead...

"Your brother appears to have met his prey here," Amos says, fingering the terrain. "And the wolf its. I believe your brother was able to shoot the wolf, but it obviously wasn't a fatal shot, because there is no body or signs of drag marks, burial, or burning."

That would mean Thomas is still alive too... if it weren't a werewolf he had been fighting, that is. They're rather notorious for devouring people, after all.

Suddenly, I feel like I'm going to be sick.

"There are signs of a man retreating in one direction and wolf prints retreating in the other," Amos adds, still studying the ground, learning all of its dirty little secrets.

"We have to follow the man's tracks," I say, standing up, my health suddenly restored.

Amos puts his hand firmly on my shoulder. "Not yet."

I pull away. "And why not? Thomas might be hurt."

He points up to the setting sun. "Night is falling. We must get somewhere more secure- there is one, possibly two werewolves in this forest."

"Thomas can't be a werewolf," I answer matter-of-factly as my mind searches for some facts to back the matter. "Um- there are no signs of torn clothing! Wouldn't torn clothing be a natural consequence of growing out of your skin?"

"True," Amos agrees, climbing a nearby tree. "Obviously, he wasn't bit. If bit, one transforms immediately and is doomed to transform during every full moon and with every outburst of anger. Some werewolves have even been known to be able to transform every night- by will or not, I'm not sure." He reaches a sturdy-looking branch far from the ground and checks it before calling down, "Can you climb?"

"I grew up in the middle of a forest," I point out as I climb up the tree to his branch, "Of course I can climb."

Amos pulls some rope out of his backpack and gestures for me to lie down. Frowning, I do, and he moves to tie me to the branch, but then I take it from him and do it myself, keeping the knot where I can easily assess it. He tugs the knot to make sure it's tight before climbing to a nearby branch and tying *himself* down.

"We're going to find my brother first thing in the morning?" I ask, studying the knot and wondering how quickly I can undo it and jump down the tree if I need to.

"In the *morning*," Amos agrees.

I force my attention away from the knot and situate my back pack as a pillow (with the weapons on the bottom). I'll stay up here for tonight; but first thing in the morning I'm looking for my brother. And until then I need to know all I can to help him. "You mentioned wolf bites like it was just *one* means of spreading lycanthropy. And I know there are, in some legends, other means- like drinking rain water out of a wolf print- but do *you* believe there are others?" He's the one who makes a living off of killing werewolves, after all.

"Yes," Amos answers. "There is at least one other, though it is much slower and less effective than a bite. In fact, many who receive it never become a wolf unless they experience a fit of intense anger."

A dark part deep inside me completely unconnected to my concern for Thomas can't help but lean forward curiously as it does every time such dark matters are discussed. "And how is this alternative to being bitten administered?"

"Through a scratch from a werewolf claw."

I suddenly feel very, very cold in a sick sort of way.

No, it can't be true. It can't be true because...

Even my desperate mind cannot find a reason why I may not, at this very moment, have lycanthropy flowing through my veins.

Chapter Four

In which I wake up in a tree, eat a sandwich, and flee to the cellar

Pain. Confusion. Fear. More pain.
Anger.

I wake with a start. With another start, I realize that I'm suspended several yards off the ground.

Carefully, I untie my bindings and situate myself. Glancing at Amos, I find that he's still asleep. I take the opportunity to untangle my hair and then run my finger along my scar... my werewolf scar?

More anger.

I shudder. Just because I may have been scratched by a werewolf doesn't make me one. I've always been a very calm, mellow girl- werewolves are supposed to be angry and fierce.

It's not me who attacked Thomas; it can't be. My clothes would be torn if I did. All logic argues that it wasn't me.

But what if it *was* me?

I repress the urge to be sick and glance at Amos again. Still sleeping. Now would be the opportune time to remove his no doubt silver-tipped sword and leave. He'll probably use it on Thomas if we find that he really has been turned. Amos would use it on *me* if he knew about my scar.

I creep over to his branch and reach to remove the sword, but then pause. All Amos has been to me is helpful, and here I am trying to steal from him and leave him defenseless in this potentially wolf-infested forest. It just isn't just.

I sigh and step back. No, I will not do that to Amos. I will stay with him and continue searching for my brother with his help. And if Thomas *is* a werewolf- or if Amos learns about my scar- well, I'm strong enough to take him down.

I gasp. That thought wasn't mine. Well, it was, but where did it come from? A sweet little Christian girl like me shouldn't think such things. And a genius such nonsense.

But what if it *isn't nonsense*? And even if it is...

Is lycanthropy taking over my mind?

~~~

"Good morning, Miss," Amos greets when he finally wakes up about two minutes after me.

"Good morning," I answer, wishing it were so.

Amos climbs down and I follow. Then he opens his backpack and removes two pieces of beef jerky. He holds one out to me.

"No thank you," I answer. "I have my own supplies." To prove my point, I remove a neatly wrapped peanut butter and jelly sandwich (just because we don't live in society doesn't mean Father doesn't still make rare stops to pick up essential staples). As much as I want the meat, it's best I don't eat it. I don't want to feed my potential lycanthropy- literally.

Together, eating our breakfasts, Amos and I follow the path the fleeing man took. I repress my questions for as long as I can so that I don't seem desperate. When I finally manage to finish my sandwich, though, I can't take it any longer. I wipe my hands on my pants. "Amos?"

"Yes?"

"If my brother does have a scratch..."

"I won't kill him if that's what you're asking. As long as he hasn't yet transformed into a wolf there is still a chance he can be helped; trained to never give in to anger. My family has helped many victims of the wolf claw overcome their lycanthropy."

I smile. There's hope for Thomas- and myself- yet.

Unless either of us have been fully transformed into werewolves, which is a possibility. My sandwich threatens to come back up, but I manage to keep it down and ask, "And if he's bitten?"

Amos looks down, but more to study his boots than to study the trail. "Then I will do my duty."

I bite my tongue. "But what if it was that girl you were worried about who was bit? Surely you wouldn't slay her."

"I wouldn't let her be bitten."

"But what if she were?"

"Then... then I would feel obliged to find a cure."

"But didn't you say that there wasn't a cure for lycanthropy?"

"There isn't as far as I know. But I would find one."

"Wouldn't my brother deserve the same right to have a chance for a cure if there were any possibility of one?"

Amos finally looks back at me, his face sympathetic. "I suppose it would depend how dangerous he would be to those around him until we found the cure. The probably *nonexistent* cure."

Since we seem to be talking in circles, I decide to change the subject before I accidentally slip and tell him that he will not be killing my brother, dangerous or not. "So, I know you came across the wolf's trail in Chicago, but surely there's more to the story than that."

"It was some party I was investigating while searching for Capone's men. Apparently, vampires enjoy moonshine as much as the next guy- that is, in others' bloodstreams. Anyway, I became aware of a werewolf in the vicinity, and when I began tracking him, I found him to be on the hunt, and I followed him here."

"Oh." I try to think of something else to ask to keep him talking and me from talking. "So, besides vampires and werewolves, are there any other creatures of legend that menace society?"

"Well, there are no other such menaces of society that I know of, but there are other creatures of legends. At least, there are faeries, which seem to be allies to the human race. There are also rumors that merfolk exist, but I've never seen one personally. They're not my business anyway. My business is vampires and werewolves."

I smile. "It's just like Father thought then: faeries, merfolk, vampires, and werewolves all coexisting with us. He'd be so pleased." Hopefully he will live long enough to find out; that thought wipes the smile off my face.

Amos looks back again. "Your father has theories on legends?"

"Yes; I'll have to introduce you-" A large, cold drop of rain lands on the bridge of my nose, and just like that I'm completely focused on panic. "We have to find Thomas before this rain washes away his trail!"

Amos nods, and we both pick up our pace.

Within moments it's raining so hard I can barely see. Amos takes my hand to prevent us from separating. I try not to enjoy it so much. It's surprisingly easy since I'm so concerned about the trail.

"I can't find any traces of Thomas in this downpour!" I cry.

"Look," Amos answers, nodding forward. "I think we may have reached his destination."

I look ahead and find my cottage. "Home! He came home." I drag Amos to the door and push inside. "Thomas!"

"Thomas?" Priscilla asks, looking up from the bow and arrow she was staring at. "Who's that?"

I close the door behind Amos and me and turn around to face the girl. "Hasn't my brother returned?"

"I don't think so," she answers, thinking hard about it, which seems to be a new thing for her. "You two are the first people I've seen since you left- besides your father, of course. Though, come to think of it, there was a strange whimpering outside earlier..."

I freeze. "Whimpering? Did you see who was doing it?"

"Well, I opened the door, but I didn't see anything. It was pretty dark out. Anyway, I've been nursing your father almost every second since you left. Except when I investigated the whimpering. And ate. And slept."

I comb my wet hair back, careful to keep the designated patch in front of my scar, trying to get my thoughts together. "How is he?"

"Oh, he's much better. I should be getting my three wishes in *no* time."

I nod. Then I turn around and begin to open the door again.

Amos grabs my hand. "Whoa- what are you doing, Miss?"

"I have to find my brother."

"No one can see in that rain and you'll be no good to him if you get pneumonia, and I have a feeling he would be very put out with both of us if you did."

I release my hold of the handle. He's right, as much as I hate to admit it- I won't be able to find anything in the downpour besides sickness; I'll just have to wait until it passes over. And hope Thomas has found shelter from both the rain and the wolf...

"So, are you going to introduce me to your gentleman friend?" Priscilla asks, giggling, of course.

"Oh, right." Father should have taught me better manners even if we do live in a remote cottage in the middle of the woods. "Priscilla, this is Amos, a boy I stumbled upon in the forest. Amos, this is Priscilla, a girl who showed up at my house the other day."

"A pleasure," Amos says, shaking Priscilla's hand.

Priscilla squeaks in perfect imitation of a mouse.

I push past both of them and hurry to Father's bedside. He's asleep, but he does look healthier than last time I saw him.

"Father?" I whisper, seeing again how much he has aged beyond his time, with gray streaks in his auburn hair and dark circles under his tired eyes.

Those eyes open and dart around. "Jane? Where are

you?"

I take his glasses from the end table and slide them onto his face.

He relaxes. "Jane, how are you? And where is Thomas?"

I bite my lip. "He still hasn't returned from hunting."

Father rubs his face. "What have I done...? Jane, what day is it today?"

"It's twenty days until my birthday."

He sighs in relief. "There's still time then."

"Father, you're being cryptic again. What is it? What's going on?"

Father sighs again, but not in relief this time. "You're a clever girl; your mind can work in ways that other minds struggle to comprehend..."

"Yes, Father. I can handle anything you need to tell me."

"But genius or not, you are still a young girl," Father adds. "A burden like this is more than you'd be able to bear."

"No, Father-" I reach up and touch my face. "Is it about my scar? I already know that it may be from a werewolf- I know now that they exist. I know I may very well have lycanthropy in my veins."

Father closes his eyes. "If only that were all- "

A wolf howls outside.

Father pales completely. "You must get to the cellar *now*."

I nod. "We *both* need to get to the cellar now." I help Father out of bed. We both hurry to the kitchen, where Priscilla is preparing Amos a snack.

"Cellar now," I order.

"Just a moment," Priscilla says, finishing a sandwich, but Amos jumps up and hurries to the cellar doors, which he swings open.

Both Romulus and Remus jump down, whimpering.

Even more freaked out than before, I lead my father to the entrance of the cellar.

"Allow me, Miss," Amos says, supporting Father down into the cellar.

I nod. Then I pull Priscilla from her work and all but toss her down before jumping down myself. Just as I close the doors and bolt them into place, I almost believe that I hear the front door of the cottage burst open.

"He shouldn't be here yet," Father whispers. "He gave me until... My sending Thomas must have angered him. Oh, what has become of my Thomas?"

I go to Father's side and lay my hand on his shoulder. "It will be all right, Father. Amos and I have been looking for Thomas, and I, for one, will not stop until I find him."

Father shakes his head sadly. His shoulders are sagging like he bears Atlas' burden.

Amos approaches us. "Excuse me, sir- I'm Amos Hood. It's my solemn duty to hunt werewolves and- anyway, I desire to help your family, but I need any information you can give me about this werewolf you fear so much. Have you met it before?"

"I- "

Father is drowned out by the sound of a large being throwing itself onto the cellar doors.

I slap my hand over my mouth to stifle a scream, and Father pales so white I'd be scared Amos would mistake him for a vampire if I wasn't already too terrified of whatever is upstairs to spare any. Priscilla attaches herself to my arm like a lamprey and Amos reaches back for his sword.

The creature bangs on our cellar doors again and again, but I'm relieved to find that the doors hold. I always thought they seemed rather thick...

I glance at Father. He prepared for this, didn't he?

"The doors will hold," Father announces, proving my theory, but not explaining how.

Amos studies him warily.

The creature above us claws at the door. Then it howls in anger.

Pain. More pain. Pain on top of pain.

"Ow," I moan, looking down at my hands. They feel like they should be bleeding, but they aren't.

The creature- wolf- *werewolf*- howls again.

Then all is silent.

"W-what now?" Priscilla whispers, shaking like a leaf (and it's her connection to my arm that is causing me to shake likewise, I'm sure).

Amos lowers his hand from his sword, but remains tense. "We say our prayers and wait the night out."

I nod, and all four of us- and even the dogs- silently look up at the cellar door with eyes so wide, my lycanthropy might mistake them for moons.

Pray, watch, wait, hope- and somehow survive this night.

Chapter Five
In which I learn the wolf can communicate in more ways than one

I hear howling in the distance. Terrified, I scan my surroundings, only to find myself standing in a part of the forest I've never been in before, with menacing shadows dancing around me.

Suddenly, Thomas darts past me.

"Thomas?" I call.

He ignores me and keeps running. I take off running after him. "Thomas!"

Then I hear the sound of something chasing us.

"Thomas!" I scream. "What's going on?!"

He doesn't answer; he probably doesn't hear me. That's the worst part of this whole situation, I think: being so terribly isolated from all help.

Even though I haven't stopped running, the thing that is chasing me passes me and then comes to a stop in front of me. It's a wolf, the same one that scarred me as a child, only much, much *bigger. It opens its mouth, which stretches large enough that I could walk in. In fact, that's what it wants me to do.*

I try to stop myself, but my feet keep moving, and I run right into that dark abyss...

I jerk awake, soaked in sweat, with a scream trapped on my lips. The room I find myself in is dark, and for a moment I wonder if maybe walking into the wolf's jaws wasn't a dream. But then my eyes adjust to the light and I find the forms of Father and Priscilla lying around me, as well as the forms of Romulus and Remus lying at my feet. Amos' form is leaning against the wall, though whether he's awake or not, I can't tell. My gaze climbs the ladder to the cellar doors and finds them still closed and sealed.

Sighing with relief, I roll over and think about the dream I just had. Terrifying as it was, it was completely different from the nightmares I've had before; with those, I was always the wolf. This was just a plain old nightmare.

I almost laugh. I can't believe it- I've actually had a *normal* nightmare. Shaking my head, I smile and return to sleep.

~~~

Pain. Anger. Hate.

I jerk awake again. So, so much hate. Never before have I felt hate, and now I know it so strongly.

"What's wrong?" Amos asks from his corner.

"I feel hate," I whisper. "But it's not *my* hate." I purse my lips; that must have sounded wrong.

Amos studies me, but I can't for the life of me figure out what he's seeing. "Are you sure?"

"I don't hate anyone and I never have," I whisper. Who was I to hate? My family? "But now I suddenly feel it, but towards no one in particular..."

"Well, sometimes when there is so much negative feeling around me, I almost feel like it's mine," he offers, but his voice hints that he's still trying to figure out whatever it is that is *really* happening to me.

I bite my lip and decide to cling to his solution even if

he doesn't quite believe it. "How do you expel those feelings? How do you ensure that they don't become your feelings, or at least keep yourself from acting upon them?"

"I pray for help and try to focus on something pure. Like waterfalls."

"And dogs?"

Amos cringes. "If you like dogs, I suppose. I've dealt with too many werewolves myself…" He glances warily at Romulus and Remus.

I bite my tongue to keep from asking how he 'dealt' with them- that probably won't help with thinking pure thoughts. Instead, I try to apply Amos' advice.

Waterfalls. Puppies. Gold. The stag. Amos.

My alien feeling subsides and I sigh in relief.

"Better?" Amos asks.

I nod.

"That was fast. You may have the impressive mind that you claim after all."

"You doubted me?"

"Would you believe a random stranger you just stumbled upon in the forest if they claimed to be a genius?"

"I don't know; you haven't made that claim yet."

Amos smirks. "Don't have to; it's a given."

I smile and self-consciously smooth down my hair. It must look terrible with the little time I've been able to spend on it these last few days…

"Do you think it's gone yet?" Priscilla asks suddenly, staring at the cellar doors with wide eyes.

"If it's still here, then at least it should be in its human form now," Amos says. "They rarely take wolf form by day except for outbursts of anger." He stands up. "All the same, you three remain here while I scan the area."

"Are you sure?" I ask.

He nods and reaches back for his sword before opening the cellar door and closing it again behind him.

I try to ignore my nervousness by finding something to do. I go to Father's side. "Father, it's time to wake up."

Father opens his eyes. "Is it dawn?"

"Yes, and the doors held firm."

"I thought they would; I painted silver on those doors."

Silver. That explains why they always gave me the willies to walk on them...

I shudder and my hands feel pained at the thought- though not as badly as last night. Then I reach up to touch my left ear- the ear opposite the side of my face with the scar. I pierced it twice and habitually wear two earrings- two to make up for the ear I can't adorn because I don't want to bring attention to that side of my face. I've worn earrings of various kinds of metal there, but never silver. Or iron either, now that I think of it, which is really quite odd.

"Do you think Amos is all right?" Priscilla asks.

Suddenly, the door bursts open and we all jump.

"It's gone," Amos announces, standing above us where we feared to find a wolf.

Moments later, we've freed ourselves from both the cellar and the house. The weather is crisp and clear- pure. It's like the forest is trying to forget the horrific events of last night.

Suddenly Priscilla sabotages its efforts by screaming.

"What is it?" Amos demands, hurrying to her side.

She points to the ground. I follow her gaze and find words clawed into the ground:

Give her to me or else.

Amos frowns and Father imitates a vampire's complexion again.

"No," Father whispers, backing away. "It's happening too fast; too fast."

Amos grabs his arm. "You need to tell me everything you know about this wolf right now, sir."

Father wordlessly reaches for my face and moves my bangs to the side, revealing the scar for all to see. For a long moment, all Amos does is stare at it, making it- and the rest of me, for that matter- feel very, very exposed.

"*Please*," Father pleads. "*Help me.*"

Amos nods.

Father sheds ten years for a moment. "Thank you."

Amos nods again and pulls his backpack closer, leaving me to believe that there was more said than I heard. "We have to take her to my family. They don't live far from here. Are you strong enough to travel, sir?"

Father nods, though he looks too weak to me. "Yes."

"Then let's go; we haven't a moment to lose."

"Wait," I say. "We're leaving the forest?"

Amos nods.

"But what about Thomas?"

"I still intend to help him if I can," Amos assures. "But you are in greater danger than you know."

Father puts his hand on my shoulder. "I would not have had Thomas go hunting if I didn't think he could take care of himself." But the fact that Father has regained the decade he lost belies his confidence.

"Don't you think that *I* can take care of myself?" I ask.

"There are some things we *all* need help overcoming," Amos answers. "Now come; we must be quick to make it to town before nightfall."

"Just a moment," I say. Then I run inside and grab the jar of money Father keeps for emergencies. I also grab a picture of Thomas, Father, Mother, and me- taken before the wolf incident and Mother's abandoning us, of course. Then I rejoin the others outside. "I'm ready."

As Father, Amos, Priscilla, the dogs, and I make our way through the forest, I try to assuage my worry for Thomas and myself with anticipation over the promise of going to town. And I try not to remember what happened the last time we left the forest, eight years ago; try not to remember the howls that seemed to be steadily nearing us and the screams that followed. Father had us sleep in a jewelry shop for the night instead of at the inn room we had rented, and then we went back home the next morning. But I will never forget the whispered conversations of how the wolf had broken into our inn room and utterly destroyed it. Was it the same wolf that scarred me or the one who burst into our very home? Are they all the same wolf? What does it even want from me?

And if anyone had died that night, is it partly my fault?

Suddenly, flash of white catches my eye, and I see the stag. Then it's gone.

"Beautiful," I breathe.

"What did you say?" Amos asks.

"Hmm?"

"Did you see something, Jane?" Father asks before turning to Amos and nervously asking, "Do you... Do you think the wolf might attack us now, before we can leave the forest?"

Priscilla gulps.

"I doubt it," Amos answers. "Besides the fact that it's day-"

"It might get angry at our attempted departure," Father points out, a distant look in his eyes, like he's remembering something unpleasant, and it doesn't take a stretch of imagination to figure out what his memory is.

So, he believes that this is the was the same wolf that followed us to the city too.

"Even if it does get angry," Amos adds, "it may not be able to change into a wolf yet. I've noticed that wolves seem to need a minimum of twelve hours between transformations."

Priscilla breathe a sigh of relief, but Father still looks nervous. "But what if it follows us out of the woods..."

"We'll be safe as long as we reach my family's safe house, which is very nearby."

Father nods and we keep walking until the trees begin to thin and I hear distant sounds of people.

I pause at what seems to be the edge of the forest. One more step and I'll be free of its confines. One more step and I'll be in the world I've longed to be a part of for so long.

You are trying to leave the forest, aren't you, my pet?

I freeze. What? How?

I was surprised at the potential for the connection myself when you begged me to spare your brother's life.

My heart becomes as cold as the rest of me. "Did you, Wolf?"

"What did you say, Jane?" Father asks.

You cannot hide from me in the outside world. Neither can you hide what you *are.*

"Did you spare my brother?" I whisper.

"Is something wrong, Miss?" Amos asks.

Who was that?

"No one," I answer.

Ah, no one. Of course. And to answer your question, your brother is gone from you forever.

"No!" I scream.

"Jane?" both Amos and Father ask in unison.

"He killed Thomas," I whisper, sinking to the ground.

The dogs whimper and lower both their ears and tails.

"Who?" Amos asks, scanning the forest.

"He's in her head," Father breaths. "The wolf. He must be. They're communicating through their shared lycanthropy. I didn't even realize that was possible."

He begged for mercy. Between his pleas and yours I almost spared him. Almost. But he challenged me, so I had to kill him.

"You *monster*," I hiss.

Amos grabs my shoulders. "Jane, look at me. Block him out. He's trying to make you angry. He's trying to turn you."

"What do I do?" I ask desperately.

I wish I could say he died quickly...

"Think of something pure," Amos answers.

Waterfalls. Puppies. Gold-

The obvious agony he suffered almost made me regret it. Almost.

I clench my fists. "It's not enough."

"Think," Amos urges. "Think about something better than the wolf."

"What?"

"Whatever is true, whatever is honorable, whatever is just, whatever is pure, whatever is lovely, whatever is commendable, if there is any excellence, if there is anything worthy of praise-"

I wish I could say I made it easier for him...

I close my eyes. What is true? The Bible. What is honorable? What Amos is doing for me. What is just? The government- most of the time.

I told him what I intend to do with you.

Uh, what is pure? Good drinking water. What is lovely? Amos. Wait, that sounded wrong.

Amos? So, this nobody has a name. I like to know the names of my prey-

What is commendable? That book I just finished the other day. Oh, there's another thing for just: finished.

I also like-

What has excellence? Stew. What is worthy of praise? This method, if it works.

Which, apparently, it does, because my head feels oddly light, like it's mine again, and the wolf's voice is gone.

I open my eyes. "He's gone. The connection is broken."

Father sighs in relief and Priscilla smiles, even though

she doesn't look like she understands exactly why.

    I smile back and turn to Amos, who is rubbing his face in relief. "I hope we're not too far away from your family's home," I say. "Because I'm really worn-" My eyes seal shut and I have the strangest sensation of falling.

Chapter Six

In which I meet Amos' family and listen to Father's theories for the umpteenth time

When I open my eyes, I find myself in an unfamiliar room. Its calming green accents prevent me from feeling endangered, though.

I sit up and find my back pack on the table next to me. I use its contents to freshen up. Then I step outside and find myself in another unfamiliar area, this time a narrow hallway.

Amos steps out of one of the other doors, his well-muscled body blocking the narrow hallway. "There you are."

"Where are we?"

"My home."

I resist the urge to take a more thorough look around the hallway to get a better idea of this boy who is helping me. "Are you sure we're safe from the wolf here?"

"The outer wall and all the doors are tinted with silver. It's kept us safe from both werewolves and vampires for years."

I nod even though it gives me the creeps to be surrounded by silver.

"Are you feeling better, Miss?" Amos asks.

"There aren't any more sinister voices in my head if that's what you mean. Where's my father?"

"Talking to my folks. Ready to meet them?"

"As long as they aren't half man, half canine carnivore, I think I can take it."

Amos smirks. "Well, at least you'll like my mom and

cousin."

"Wait, your dad's a werewolf?"

Amos smiles slightly, like he finds my words amusing but doesn't want to offend me, and shakes his head. "No, but he sure looks like one." He reopens the door he had just come through, revealing a dining room. Five people are sitting around a table, talking and eating: Father, Priscilla, and three strangers.

"Jane, meet my family," Amos says, gesturing to the strangers: a man, a woman, and a girl perhaps slightly younger than I. "My father, Arthur Hood; my mother, Aurora Hood; and my cousin, Debra Hood. Everyone, this is Jane Delane."

Mr. Hood, a large man with rather longish blonde hair and a full beard, nods.

I nod back before turning to the cousin. Debra's dirty blonde hair is shorter than mine but still too long to be fashionable, though her clothes are much more stylish than mine- even if she *is* wearing an ancient-looking red cloak. She studies me as curiously as I study her.

I suddenly become very aware of my brother's hand-me-downs, which are no good for visiting- or really anything besides stomping around in the woods. Then I mentally scold myself. Thomas may very well be dead; I should be thankful that I still have this small piece of him.

Thomas...

"So you went to slay a werewolf and brought back a girl, Amos?" Debra asks. "I should have expected as much after all your bragging."

"I think it's only fair to point out that I also brought

home her father and the girl who showed up at her house," Amos answers. "Also, two dogs." He glances distrustfully at Romulus and Remus, lying in the other side of the kitchen.

"Oh, quiet, Debra," Mrs. Hood, a demure woman with small features and a halo of blonde hair, scolds lightly. "Don't embarrass Amos in front of the first girl he's ever brought home."

Amos clears his throat, avoiding looking my way. "Actually second; don't forget Priscilla over there."

"Hi," Priscilla greets.

Debra shakes her head.

I study Debra. This must be the girl he was worried about the wolf hunting. His cousin. What a relief.

"How are you feeling, Jane?" Father asks.

I smile. "Much better. And you?"

Father nods, though I can still see a hint of sadness in his eyes despite the fact that he seems to be denying it.

"That's wonderful," Mrs. Hood says. "Go ahead and take a seat and start eating."

"Thank you," I answer, obeying. I take a bite of something wonderful and find myself hard-pressed to keep from shoveling it all into my mouth at once. When did I last eat? I feel like a ravenous wolf.

Oh, dear; my stomach seems to have succumbed to the lycanthropy.

Mr. Hood studies me like he knows my thoughts. "Would you show us the scar, Miss Delane?"

My appetite diminishes slightly, but I obediently push my bangs aside.

Mr. Hood nods. "That is indeed a werewolf claw mark.

I've seen them many times before."

I nod slowly, my appetite completely gone now.

"And I assure you, everyone with those scars who sought help from us has recovered," he adds. "One can always overcome the lycanthropy of a scratch as long as one desires to."

"Desires to?"

"There are those who would rather be werewolves than not. Those are beyond all help."

I do a quick mental check. I want to be cured of lycanthropy, right? Of course I do. I certainly don't want to become a wolf. How strange would that be? Let alone terrifying...

"We can help you," Mrs. Hood quickly assures. "We always begin by sharing our tales." She turns to her husband.

Mr. Hood nods. "I was once a poor factory boy who worked in bad conditions and often went to bed hungry. Then one day a man came to me and told me he was my faerie godfather and would grant me three wishes. He took me under his wing, so to speak, and showed me how to gain the trust of my fellow workers and unify them into a successful strike for better pay and conditions. However, that only satisfied two of my three wishes. For my third wish, my faerie godfather- Merlin II- led me to a decrepit house. There I found Aurora in a coma because her drunken uncle had beaten her."

Mrs. Hood glances down at her lap. "I accidentally broke the heirloom spinning wheel."

"I took her away from there," Mr. Hood adds, "and begged Merlin II to use the magic he claimed to poses to wake her. He warned me that by using the magic, he'd put me on the radar of certain other creatures: vampires, werewolves, rogue faeries, and merfolk, but I insisted. So, he gave me an article of clothing woven on a spinning wheel to cure her, she awoke, and we soon married. Then Merlin II gave me careful instructions and information for battling monsters before he disappeared from my life, and I've made it my life's work to use that knowledge to protect the rest of mankind from the monsters of their nightmares."

"Whoa," Priscilla says. "I didn't even *think* to make monster-hunting one of my wishes."

Father, who had been rubbing his chin through the entire story, finally says what I know he's been itching to say since they began their tale. "How interesting that your names and stories echo the legends of King Arthur and Sleeping Beauty."

"Just a coincidence, I suppose, Old Sport," Mr. Hood answers.

"Maybe," Father agrees, "but a coincidence with a reason. I study legends and I've found that they fall into three categories. There are Real Legends, stories that exist in almost every single culture around the world because every culture has been affected by them and have had ancestors pass down eyewitness stories of those things, though a little garbled- like the creation story, a global flood, and God."

If any of the Hoods are surprised at Father for bringing God into the conversation, they don't show it. Priscilla, however, says, "Wow."

"The second category of legends is the type I think

you will find especially interesting," Father adds. "I call them Echo Legends, because almost every culture has a similar legend or faerie-tale of those certain types. For instance, almost every culture has a tale of an underprivileged girl who goes from rags to riches, from loneliness to a royal marriage- sometimes with faerie help and step-family issues- that I call the Cinderella type."

I lean back. Heard this a thousand times.

"Then there is its counterpart where a boy goes from rags to riches, from the unknown to power because of his bravery. Sometimes this happens with a magician's or a prophet's aid, like with you, and unlike with you, there is often great relationship distress. I call this type King Arthur. Those two stories are common in various forms because everyone dreams of those becoming *their* stories. Also, those story types actually happen sometimes and keep others' hopes and dreams alive. The Biblical Ruth was a Cinderella and the Biblical King David was a King Arthur. Also, you, Arthur. And my own wife Ellen was a Cinderella."

I blink. Father has never mentioned Mother in his theory like that before.

"You seem very confident in your theory," Amos says. "But there are so many other different faerie-tales. How do you explain those?"

"I've found that there are at least three other types," Father answers. "There's the Sleeping Beauty type- this reminds me of you, Aurora- where a maiden is kidnapped by a witch, er, evil individual or has a spell put over her- usually sleep- or sometimes both. Examples of this Echo Legend are, of course, Sleeping Beauty, as well as Snow White, and Rapunzel, all of which represent how women are often mistreated but promises that true love is waiting for them."

Priscilla sighs.

"Then there's the Little Red Riding Hood type, where a child ventures into the woods and faces a scary and often sinister individual. Examples are, obviously, Little Red Riding Hood, as well as Hansel and Gretel and Goldilocks. Personally, I believe this type of story symbolizes facing one's fears and coming of age. A third Echo Legend is the Robin Hood type, which is when a man steals from the rich to give to the poor, or is simply a noble fugitive of the authority- also rather similar to King David. As for the origin of those stories, what downtrodden people don't dream of such an individual?"

Now Priscilla suddenly seems about as bored as myself and yawns. "So many types.

"Going beyond types," Debra agrees attentively, "what is the third *category* of legends?"

"Ah, the third category is what I call the Shadow Legends. They are the legends that almost every culture has because all fear them: devious faeries, tempting mermaids, bloodthirsty vampires, and ravenous wolves."

Amos shrugs to show that he's very familiar with at least half of those creatures.

"Modern experts attribute these creatures that all cultures fear in some form- like sirens or werecats- as fear inspired mistakes that every culture has made. Manatees were thought to be mermaids, rabies assumed to be vampirism, and so on. Of course, we all know those mistakes were made because people were trying to understand the threats that they all knew to be true."

I self-consciously touch my scar.

"What about ghosts?" Debra asks. "Are they true? Because almost every culture has a legend about ghosts."

"Ghosts are not real," Father answers. "Ghosts are mankind's attempt to understand the afterlife, the great unknown, just as old wives' tales are attempts to make reason come from nonsense."

Debra shakes her head. "Where were you, sir, when I was seven and Amos was always trying to frighten me with ghost stories?"

Amos chuckles and I find myself laughing too. How lovely to find laughter despite the last couple of days; to find solace after the horror of the woods.

If only Thomas were here too.

Laughter dies in my throat and goes to a destiny that isn't ghosting. Like Thomas.

"Well, now that I know that there really aren't such things as ghosts, I'm brave enough to face the real world," Debra adds suddenly. "Maybe even help Amos with his hunting-"

"We've talked about this already, Debra," Mr. Hood scolds. "Don't open the discussion again. Now be a good girl and make our guests feel welcome."

Debra narrows her eyes and studies her plate, which surprisingly enough has quite the opposite effect of making me feel welcome.

Mrs. Hood blushes at her niece's behavior before

standing up. "Who would like seconds?"

"I would," I answer, since apparently my appetite has returned, along with my hope of overcoming this lycanthropy. Now if only Thomas will return to me...

~~~

I study a shelf of antiques likes Grecian pots, scrolls, and an ancient but stunning silver dagger on a stand. There are also some more modern decorations, like china plates, postcards from several different states (but all signed by Amos), and a pen knife on a stand matching the silver dagger's. There is also a framed photograph of Mr. and Mrs. Hood, Amos, and Debra from a few years ago. I say a few years ago because this Amos can't be older than twelve in this picture, with his hair trimmed into an adorable bowl cut.

"I see you found the family treasures," someone says behind me.

I turn around and find Amos himself.

I fight a blush and gesture to the photograph. "How old were you?"

"Twelve."

I smile. Knew it. "What was it like? Being twelve in your family? Did you know about werewolves and stuff then?"

Amos joins me at the table and picks up the picture, smiling a sad sort of smile. "Yes. I've known about such things since I was very young. It wasn't supposed to be like that though." He puts the picture back down.

"What do you mean?"

"I had a very rude awakening to the creatures that live in the shadows." He says this with an air of finality, and I know he has dropped the subject, and I can't help but be a little curious.

I had a very rude awakening too, but it was a very long time in happening. It began with the wolf scratching me, continued through years of strange images and the eeriest feeling that I was being watched, all the way to the present when I've finally had my last assurances that the shadows were just shadows completely torn away, and I've come to realize that it's actually safety and security that are the myths, not werewolves.

I shake such thoughts away. Then, awkwardly, I reach out to touch the beautiful dagger, but then shiver and pull back, feeling even more awkward.

"So, what was it like for you when you were twelve, Miss?" Amos asks, kindly not commenting.

I shrug. "Oh, nothing particularly interesting. It was just me, my father, and Thomas in our cottage in the middle of nowhere."

"That actually sounds quite interesting."

"It really wasn't."

Amos smiles wryly. "I'd still like to learn more."

I blush and look away.

"You almost seem like a girl from out of one of your father's theories on legends," Amos adds.

"But which am I? The child in the woods or the creature of the shadows?"

"I was thinking more along the lines of captive maiden."

"Oh..." I search for something to say. "Thank you for

all that you're doing for me and my family."

"Think nothing of it. It is our *privileged* duty."

"Amos!" Debra calls.

"Excuse me, Miss," Amos adds before going to his cousin.

I watch him go and then study his picture with a sad sort of smile, wondering what sadness tried to steal the smile from Amos' young face.

Chapter Seven
In which I dream, dread, and decide to do something drastic

I stand at the edge of the woods, looking eye to eye with a black wolf.

"I didn't mean what I said about your brother," the wolf says.

I don't answer, hoping and dreading in the same moment.

"I could not disregard your plea so blatantly," the wolf adds. "We are connected, you and I, whether you want to believe it or not."

Manipulating our connection, I scan his mind for signs of lying and find none. "My brother is alive?"

"If it would please you, I will show you where he is."

I nod. "It would please me greatly."

Suddenly, we aren't two poisoned creatures in a forest like before. Instead, I'm looking through yellow eyes at a city scene. By the Statue of Liberty in the background, I know that it must be New York City.

The wolf's eyes- and mine- focus on an individual making his way through the crowd with his head down. Despite that, and the hat low over the individual's face, I still recognize him as Thomas.

I have to go to him. Whatever it takes.

I begin to wake up, but not before I hear the wolf think, "Now that would please me greatly."

I wake up in cold sweat. Thomas is alive. Dream or not, it meant something. And it means that my brother is in New York City. As is the wolf. And he wants me there too.

Studying my boots as I summon the energy to put them on, I ponder the choice before me: safety here with the Hoods, or danger there with my beloved brother.

~~~

Despite my dream, I smile prettily while I breakfast with the Hoods.

"We have an expert in anger suppression on his way here," Mr. Hood tells me. "You will be beyond the throes of lycanthropy in no time."

I keep my smile in place and nod. Maybe they will have me again when I return- if I return. Or maybe they'll hate me. But Thomas comes first.

Especially since I may very well be too far gone already.

"Speaking of all this lycanthropy business," Debra begins. "Perhaps I could accompany Amos the next time he goes out; just to help find Jane's brother. Surely *that's* safe enough."

Amos shakes his head.

"I'm afraid that that's out of the question, young lady," Mr. Hood answers sternly.

"But why?" she demands. "Is it because I'm a *girl*? Because I'm just as trained as Amos is; I've been practicing ever since I came here to live with you."

"Sweetheart, you know why we can't let you go," Mrs. Hood says.

"No," Debra retorts, pushing away from the table and standing up. "I just know why you *pretend* you can't let me go." With that she storms away.

It's a good thing that Debra is obviously free of lycanthropy or else she would no doubt have transformed by now.

Mrs. Hood blushes and says, "Girls of a certain age, you know-" She notices me and blushes deeper.

"No, I understand," I assure, lightheartedly. "My brother was just like that at her age..." My brother.

I *will* find him.

After breakfast, I return to the table of family treasures. I smile at the photo again before turning once more to the silver dagger. As I will be facing a werewolf in the near future, I will be needing a weapon of silver. I only hope the Hoods will forgive me someday.

I remove my own ordinary dagger from my backpack and unsheathe it. Then I grit my teeth and reach for the silver dagger.

Thankfully, the handle isn't made of silver, and I grasp it without pain. Then I quickly put it into my own sheathe and place that into my backpack. Finally, I put my plain dagger on the stand and hope no one will notice.

"There you are."

I startle and turn around to find Debra.

"Uh, hi," I greet nervously.

"I'm sorry I haven't talked with you much," she adds, "but I've been really busy studying and training. In case they ever *do* finally agree to let me help rid society of werewolves and the like, you know."

I purse my lips to keep them from spreading into a guilty smile. "Oh. Okay."

Debra studies me, like she's trying to figure something

out about me. Whatever her judgment is, she doesn't show it. Instead, she asks, "What was it like?"

"What like?"

"Facing the wolf."

"Oh." I laugh nervously and hope to heaven that she doesn't notice the different dagger on the stand. "It was terrifying. I never want to go anywhere without silver. Except I hate silver. It's complicated."

Debra nods like she wants me to think she understands even though she never could, which is fine with me as long as she doesn't understand that I'm babbling because I'm scared of being caught. "Uh-huh. And what was it like growing up? Were you sheltered like I was?"

I almost laugh. "Was I sheltered? This is the first time I've left my home in eight years."

"Oh. I know the feeling." This time, I think she really does. "What's it like being on the outside now?"

"Not like I was expecting. I was rather hoping there would be more friends, shopping, and parties- and fewer werewolves."

"I've always dreamed of finding the werewolves and slaying them. But no one will let me. They want me to focus on, well, friends, shopping, and parties instead."

"Want to trade?"

"Very much." Her eyes fall on my dagger lying on her family's table and I hold my breath, waiting for her to say something. However, if she notices anything, she certainly doesn't show it; her face remains completely emotionless as she says, "Well, I suppose I'll be returning to my studies and training." With that, she leaves, her red cloak giving her the effect of a dramatic exit.

I release my breath and quickly leave the room in search of my father.

After searching the house, I finally find a library- and, naturally, my father, relaxing with the dogs lying at his feet.

"Are you feeling better, Father?" I ask.

He nods, though his weary eyes belie his words and he reclines heavily on a sofa. "I know these people will take care of you, Jane. I just wish Thomas were..."

"Thomas is alive," I whisper. "He's in New York."

"How do you know?"

"I just do."

Father shakes his head. "Is it because of what that wolf did to you?"

I nod sheepishly, feeling like a kid caught with my hand in the cookie jar. "And, Father, you don't have to hide from me what it wants of me. I think... I think I know."

My mind, after all, is a powerful thing. I'd be an impressive weapon in the hands- paws- of a werewolf if I were to succumb to lycanthropy myself. And with things being as they are now, I won't ever be safe, even here. As long as the creature can talk to me, even just telepathically, I'll never be safe. That's why I need to go face the wolf- to save Thomas and my own mind.

"I'm so sorry, Janie," Father says. "I had hoped the issue would be taken care of before you figured it out." His eyes begin to droop.

I clear my throat. "And I will protect myself to the best of my abilities. But I have to... I mean, I need to... Would you give me your blessing to...?"

Father's head lolls backwards.

Okay, so, I admit I was really beating around the bush there, but falling asleep seems a bit extreme.

I shake my head and lean towards him. "I hope you have good dreams," I whisper, kissing him on the forehead. "And I hope you'll understand my actions when you wake. My mind will never be safe as long as it's connected to the wolf, so it's simply better that I face him now attempting to rescue Thomas rather than waiting until the wolf finally makes me so angry I turn."

Sighing, I straighten up and leave the room. There, I find Priscilla with her ear against the wall.

She quickly straightens up. "I wasn't eavesdropping."

I don't have time to bother with her so I just order, "Take care of my father."

She nods hurriedly and I walk past her.

Finally, I reach the front door, which is burdened by so many locks and bolts that the door looks almost comical. Thankfully, I'm clever.

Closing the door again behind me, I find myself alone in the outside I've longed so long to be a part of. People bustle around, bicycles whiz by, and the occasional car drives down the streets. Here I am at long last. I just never thought I'd feel so alone when I joined civilization. Or that I'd be leaving behind Father to search for Thomas. And I definitely didn't think there would be a werewolf out there somewhere hunting for me.

I push away the facts and focus on my mission pure and simple: finding a taxi cab.

Chapter Eight
In which I am found by Amos, make a likely alliance, and visit two churches

"I knew you would see it my way" the wolf says.

"No, I see it my *way, which just so happens to be* parallel *to your way."*

The wolf laughs. "I'm so glad you turned out to be so clever, my pet."

I freeze. Pet? I'll never be his pet. I'd sooner die. "Go. Now. Leave me alone."

He grins, revealing his teeth. "If that's what you think you want..."

I wake up to the feeling that I'm being watched.

Sitting up, I scan the church I had found refuge in last night. After all, churches are supposedly off-limits to werewolves (though apparently not to dreams of werewolves). Besides, I wanted to get away from the strangeness of the outside world I had dreamed of for so long- and the crass string (though it was more of a rope) of words my cabbie uttered every time someone cut him off, as well as the odd looks I got from complete strangers because of my boyish clothes and long hair.

My eyes finally find the one intruding my solace. Amos Hood is sitting erect on the pew opposite mine. He does not look happy.

And, terrible as it is to think in a church, not happy is a becoming look on him.

"Amos," I greet, running a hand through my hair. "What a surprise." Though I really *should* be getting used to this, considering this is the *fourth* time I've awakened to him being near.

"Miss Delane," he answers coolly, "do you have even the *slightest* idea the danger you and Debra are traipsing off to meet?"

"Why, yes I do, *sir*. I was in the cellar with you when the wolf- wait; what about Debra?"

"She accompanied you, didn't she?"

"No..."

"Don't toy with me. My cousin's safety is at stake, and that does not please me one whit."

I frown. "I assure you, I'm not playing any games. I told no one of my departure except my father, who was asleep. Though..." I cringe.

"Though what?"

"Though Priscilla might have overheard our conversation..."

Amos pulls at his face like he wants to pull it off, which would be a shame, really. "Debra must have heard it from her... She's always longed to hunt for legends with me because a werewolf murdered her parents, but it is *because* of that fact that she mustn't."

"A werewolf murdered her parents?"

He cringes, and I know that this must have been the bit of bad history that awakened him to the truth that monsters aren't myths. "Yes. Merlin was right when he said that the monsters would be attracted to the magic he used to wake my mother. My father prepared himself and told his brother to do the same but my uncle refused to follow his instructions to fortify his house."

"Why?" I ask. If Thomas were to tell me to fortify against werewolves, I would- I *did*.

Amos shrugs. "Both disbelief and jealousy over Father's new-found good fortune."

I close my eyes, imagining the grief they must have suffered. "I'm so sorry."

Amos shakes his head and stands up. "Apologies are useless right now. I need to take you back so I can go find my foolish cousin who is even now in grave danger."

I stand up too. "No. You and I must *both* go after your cousin. If she didn't stop for rest like I did, she must be almost to New York by now. You can't waste any time on me."

Amos' jaw clenches. "Do you even realize what the wolf wants from you?"

I nod solemnly. "But he needs to be faced. Your cousin..." My brother. My mind.

He groans. "Fine. Since time is of the essence, you'll have to stay with me until I've found my cousin and we can all return to relative safety. And if we face the wolf, as we most certainly shall, be assured that I will kill it- or any other monster- before it can touch you again."

Including Thomas if he's turned. Shivers run down my spine.

"However," he adds, "in order for you to be under my protection, you must follow my orders. Every. Single. One. Understand?"

I nod. "I will obey your every order while under your protection."

Amos nods back and then turns towards the exit.

Before I follow his lead, I add under my breath, "*Except* any rules regarding Thomas. I will not let you hurt him, whatever it takes. Even if it will put me outside of your protection."

"Are you coming, Miss?" Amos calls from the door.

"Yes," I answer, pleased that we've come to a mutual understanding.

~~~

"Where can I take you two?" a spry-looking, though wheezy-sounding elderly man inside the taxi cab asks.

"The city limits," Amos answers coolly, tossing him a coin. "And that's all you need to know."

The cabbie's eyes widen. "Ah, *elopers*. Don't worry; I drive a couple escaping the city jus' about every week. Never been caught yet."

Amos mutters something under his breath and climbs into the cab. I, however, stay where I am.

"We're not eloping," I correct.

"Don't worry, little Missie," the cabbie assures. "I won't be telling nobody your little secret."

"No, you're mistaken. We're not eloping."

The cabbie nods very slowly. "You really don't have to worry about me knowing, Missie."

Before I can refute him again, Amos grabs my hand and pulls me into the carriage with him.

"Let him believe what he wants," Amos whispers. "It's better that way."

"But it's not true. I'd never elope with you." All right, so maybe *that* might be stretching the truth slightly, but I can't have him thinking otherwise now can I?

"Be assured that the feeling is mutual, Miss."

I look away before he realizes just how un-mutual it is.

It's not his fault that he's the first unrelated young man I've ever met, after all.

"Lucky you got a girl with long hair," our cabbie says as he starts the team. "I haven't seen one of 'em with long hair since bobs got stylish."

I self-consciously reach up to touch my unfashionable hair.

"Now, you keep scissors away from her, you hear?" he adds.

"Yes, yes, of course," Amos agrees, ignoring both him and me in favor of the cab window. I get the feeling that he still hasn't forgiven me for running away.

"And that's a mighty fine hat on yer head, laddie," our cabbie says cheerfully. "Can't say I've ever seen one like it, but it looks to be a good hat. Where'd you git it?"

Amos frowns ever so slightly before plastering on a fake smile and taking both my hands in his. "I just had the most wonderful idea, Darling Dearest. To make up for your lack of a finer wedding dress, you could weave flowers into your long locks."

Five things become apparent to me in that moment: one, Amos is holding my hands; two, he doesn't want anyone knowing something about that hat; three, he's holding my hands (it bears repeating); four, the cabbie is eating this all up; and five, Amos is definitely still angry with me.

I decide to ask about the hat later. But I'll try to fix his anger now. Neither Father nor Thomas was ever able to stay angry with me when I used my 'sweet girl' face, perfected from early childhood. I'm sure it would work on Amos too.

I tilt my head, press my lips together, and bat my eyelashes. "That sounds absolutely perfect, darling dearest."

Amos' eyes widen and he opens his mouth ever so slightly, but then the cab lurches to a stop, sending us both to the ground.

"Sorry 'bout that," our cabbie calls. "An aggressive milk man just cut me off."

Amos and I awkwardly attempt to untangle ourselves. In the process, Amos accidentally brushes my scar.

Anger. Anger and pain, but mostly anger.

I shudder.

"I'm sorry," Amos says, suddenly gentle. He helps me back into my seat before seating himself several inches away from me.

I turn away and focus my attention on the scenes outside my window, but I don't really see. Our cabbie continues chattering, but I don't really hear. All I can seem to focus on is Amos sitting as far from me as he can and the burning embarrassment from *so* many causes.

~~~

"Here we are," our cabbie announces, parking the cab at the fringes of the city.

"Thank you," Amos says, moving to the door. "Come on, darling; we can walk from here."

"Wait, you don't have any other means of transportation ready?" our cabbie asks.

"No-"

"Then I must insist that I keep driving you; can't have

the lady walking overly long. And the chapel is still some ways..."

"That's very kind of you, sir-" Amos begins.

"I know," he agrees, revving the engine again.

Amos sighs and shakes his head before sitting back down.

When our extended cab ride finally comes to a stop, the sun is setting and night is preparing to pounce while the sun is weak.

I shudder. I never used to be afraid of the dark before. Stupid wolf.

"I'm afeared that this is the farthest I can go," our cabbie says, opening the door for us. "There's a church just a couple blocks away, just so you know. They'll marry you for real cheap with no questions asked."

"We're not-" I begin.

"Thank you," Amos interrupts, tipping the cabbie. Then he starts walking towards the church.

I sigh and then hurry to keep pace with him. "Aren't we going to keep searching? There really isn't time to elope with your cousin in trouble like that."

Amos raises an eyebrow. "I thought you'd never elope with me."

"Of course I wouldn't."

Amos shakes his head. "You are a very unusual girl, Jane. Not to worry, though; we are simply staying the night there. Desperate as I am to find my cousin, traveling at night is just begging an attack from mature werewolves and about any kind of vampires. Especially with my exposure to magic and your exposure to lycanthropy. And as you already seem to know, churches are as effective as silver in keeping out werewolves. Sacred ground and all that."

I nod and resist the urge to touch my scar.

In the church powder room, I freshen up and change into a more comfortable outfit. When I rejoin Amos, he hands me a sandwich and a canteen of water.

After a quick bless-this-food prayer (I need all the help I can get), I ask, "Why were you so desperate to keep our cabbie from learning anything about your strange hat?"

"The same reasons I'm not telling you now," Amos answers. "Now, for a more important question: what led you to run away?"

"I'll tell you only if you agree to tell me how you managed to find me- that is, unless you want to change your mind and tell me the truth about the hat."

"Agreed. Though, it really wasn't hard to follow the sightings of the auburn Rapunzel."

I finger the tips of my hair. "I really should cut it."

Amos smiles slightly and shakes his head. "I'm afraid that I've been charged to keep scissors away from you, Miss. Besides, I hate waste."

I scowl at him, but inwardly decide to keep my hair long. If Amos likes it, well...

"Now tell me why you left," he orders, suddenly serious again.

I try to ignore the janitor who begins dusting in the corner. Thankfully, he ignores us too.

"The wolf spoke to me through our connection again," I whisper. "He showed me my brother. He's alive. I need to find him just as you need to find your cousin."

Amos rubs his face. "I see."

"I know it was reckless," I add. "But I thought Thomas was dead- it told me he was. And then it showed me my brother... Why do you think it is playing with me like that?"

"I don't know," Amos says dryly. "Psychopath werewolves are extremely rare."

"I think the better term is 'manic depression'."

"Now those are much more common. All werewolves have a 'split personality,' so to speak."

I resist the urge to touch my scar again. Am I doomed to become a manically depressed psychopath? "Surely they aren't *all* bad?"

Amos studies me for a moment before answering, "Well, I don't want to be hasty about making any generalizations, but I've never met a good werewolf."

"Well, I suppose the same could be said about people, and yet it's considered quite rude to go around killing them."

To his credit, Amos doesn't look offended. "It's different with werewolves. I have to kill them for others' safety. Their natural instinct is to devour people."

I bring my hand to my mouth in horror, feeling suddenly very sick to my stomach.

"Sometimes I think that isn't what they truly want, but their animal side knows no boundaries." Amos shakes his head, lost in thought. "Sometimes they beg me to put them out of their misery."

I shudder. Poor Thomas. Poor me. Poor wolf even.

"Most of the time, though, they want to eat me as much as I want to kill them." Amos seems to notice me again and frowns. "I'm sorry; I shouldn't be telling you these things."

"No... it's okay..." Because what if he's wrong about werewolves? What if these are just the ones that he finds? Maybe- just maybe- there are others out there leading borderline normal lives- with clean consciences- amongst completely normal people. Maybe there's hope for Thomas and me yet.

Amos doesn't look convinced that any of it is okay as he says, "Get some sleep." Then he stretches out on his pew, placing his hands under his head. His eyes have a mixture of the lost innocence of a child and the heavy burdens of the elderly.

Poor Amos.

Ignoring the janitor now sweeping the floor, I stretch out on my own pew and close my eyes. There is a refreshing lack of wolf in my dreams- but a disturbing surplus of Amos.

Chapter Nine
In which I flirt with evil and then return to church

Fire. Burning. Burning Fire. Burning me. Pain. So much pain. My *pain, for once. Burning pain.*

Feverishly, I wake up to a slight burning sensation and find myself wearing a delicate silver bracelet attached to the pew leg by a delicate silver chain.

Amos is nowhere to be seen but there is, however, a note taped to the pew in front of me that says: *If you wake up before I return, be assured that I will return at dawn. I apologize about the silver, but it's safer out here for me than for you. Remember not to get angry. Your acquaintance, Amos.*

I narrow my eyes. Don't get angry, huh? Well, too late for that.

My scar begins to burn and my heart ices over with fear to counteract it. I mustn't give in to anger or else all is lost.

Desperate to focus on anything but my anger, I glance down at my wrist. The bracelet is pretty loose; if I dared, I could squeeze my hand all the way through.

I take a deep breath and pull. The silver bracelet touches the top of my hand as I slide it off, making my whole hand feel as though it's on fire. With a gasp and a last painful tug, though, my hand is free.

Breathing hard, I wipe away the perspiration that collected on my forehead. At least my distraction was effective- I'm now in too much pain to bother being angry.

You're hurt.

A chill goes down my spine. The wolf. "Get out of my head," I order. My brief moment of anger must have been enough to link us despite my being fully awake- not asleep or vulnerable- and on sacred ground.

You know as well as I that I am not 'in your head.' Our minds are simply connected.

"You know as well as I that I don't care what you call it- just get out of my head!"

Who hurt you?

"Besides you? None of your business, wolf."

But it is. If someone hurt you, then I must hurt them.

I block out all thoughts to keep him from learning anything about- don't think it!

Don't think what?

"Just get out of my head!"

Single-minded little one, aren't you? But, my pet, I want to help you.

"I don't want any of your 'help'!"

Then I suppose you know your way to New York? Perhaps you've found some other guide to lead you to your brother?

I rub my still-burning wrist. "Actually, I haven't."

Never fret, Dear One. Simply tell me your location and I will mentally guide you to your brother. I am nothing if not helpful.

"Swallow your lies and your 'Dear Ones,'" I order before wondering if that was the best turn of phrase to use. But he's right about my needing a guide...

Shaking my head- all my logic must be making me go mad- I make sure that it is dawn and that Amos isn't nearby. The wolf won't be able to touch me now- and I won't let Amos touch me again. Then I take a deep breath. "I'm in Harrisburg, Pennsylvania. Now be a good doggie and tell me how to find you so I can kill you."

The wolf laughs. *I find your spunk endearing. You really slay me. Now, my pet, thank you ever so much for allowing me to 'lend a paw.'*

I grit my teeth and step outside the shelter of the church.

~~~

I pause at the edge of a forest. I've followed the wolf's directions this far, but to go into unfamiliar woods at his urging?

You're hesitating.

"Of course I am. You're probably waiting for me in the heart of the forest."

That's ridiculous; I am in New York. You and I both know that."

I sense no lies about him, but I still don't trust him.

Besides, you're *the most dangerous one between us, with your dagger of silver.*

"Says the one with the mouthful of teeth-"

You have teeth too.

"My canines are nothing compared to yours, canine. And why do you think I have a silver dagger anyway?"

I can sense it on you just as you are aware of it with every step you take. Silver calls to us as much as death calls to mortals.

I wrap my arms around myself. "I'm still not entering those woods."

But it's the shortcut.

"Then show me the long cut." Carrying silver or not, I'm not ready to face death yet, no matter how much beckons.

Very well...

Soon I am walking a well-worn road. Though there are not many people around, I feel infinitely safer here where I can call for help, or at least see the danger coming.

Happy?

"I'd be much happier if this ridiculous farce were over and done with."

What farce?

"You know very well what I mean: your leading me into your tap."

I am merely leading you to where you belong.

"Like I said: ridiculous."

There's nothing ridiculous about how I feel about you, my pet.

"What? Hungry?"

The wolf laughs. *I do enjoy your spunk. I am so glad I chose you. Do you know why I chose you?*

"Yes. You want my mind to make me a weapon, you horrible monster."

You are a confused, little one. But believe what you want for now, my pet. Except that I chose you for your mind- that's just too wrong. Truthfully, I chose you for your eyes. They remind me of the moon with their size and color. You were beautiful even as a child, and you have grown more beautiful with each passing year.

I freeze. "You've been watching me grow up?"

I allowed your father to continue raising you until your seventeenth birthday, but I could never stay away for long. I visited at least once a year, being sure your father remembered to take good care of you and never take you from the safety of the woods until I could come for you.

So many things swirl through my head, but I can't seem to put the pieces together. "Why? Why all this?"

Your beauty. Your brain. Your spunk. And I especially like your idea about being a weapon. You will indeed be deadly.

"But I was just a child," I whisper. "A child. How could you look at a child and think it'd be deadly?" None of this is making sense...

Age isn't an issue with me. I could wait for you for an eternity if I had to. But you can't. So, on the eve of your seventeenth birthday either you will come to me or I will come to you, and I will grant you the gift of immortality.

"Immortality?" I can't think. Nothing's making sense. Rhyme and reason have deserted me. "But why?!"

The wolf laughs and then goes silent.

I pull at my hair, trying to put together the puzzle; trying to fix my life. But all I find is confusion and hopelessness. I'm tempted to sink to my knees in despair, but then a man dressed as a farmer drives by in a Ford. I hurry to keep pace with him.

"Please, sir, may I ride with you?" I call. I have to get to civilization again; I can't be alone anymore.

Thankfully, the man hears me and comes to a halting stop. "Of course, Ma'am."

"Thank you," I breathe, climbing up into the seat next to his. He must have a daughter at home, bless his heart.

The man revs his engine and we're off.

I find solace from the chaotic confusion of my life by thinking of nothing at all.

~~~

Are you still awake, my pet?

"Of course I'm still awake," I mutter, ignoring the disturbed look the driver- Scott- is giving me. "It's still day." Though, the sun is beginning to set... I shudder.

You still have a long trip ahead of you, dear one. Go ahead and rest your eyes. Guten nacht, guten nacht, guten nacht, little dear one-

"Are you *singing* to me?" I demand.

"No, ma'am," Scott answers, giving me a strange look.

Yes...

"Stop it," I order. "It was one thing when you were giving me directions, but I draw the line at having a wolf-man singing German lullabies in my head."

Scott gulps nervously and glances around for help.

Ah, but I haven't sung for so long, my pet.

"Oh, trust me, I can tell."

Please.

"The line has been drawn."

In that case, I must break the connection now. There are... things that I must attend to.

"Don't let me get in the way then. And drop the pet names already!"

My mind suddenly feels woozy, like I've been focused on something for so long, and the object of my focus has been snatched away.

Dazed, I scan my surroundings. Thankfully, I'm in a small town of sorts, not the forest. No doubt I'll be able to find a church. Sure, I want to face the wolf, but not at night, and not after he's been in my head all day. I feel to... vulnerable. "I'm getting off here," I tell Scott.

He's only too eager to have the crazy girl out of his car.

I don't have to walk far to find an impressive-looking cathedral. And in case they don't take me in, a small, rather rustic chapel stands just across the street from it.

At the cathedral, I'm greeted by an elderly man in ornate robes.

"Excuse me," I greet, using my innocent face, "may I please stay the night here? I have nowhere else to go..."

"Of course," the man wheezes. "We house travelers often. Just moments ago a young man found shelter here- "

I pause. "A young man? Did he, by any chance, have a strange hat?"

The man frowns, his lips trembling at the exhausting task of remembering something. "He... he did, actually. I've never seen anything like it."

I sigh. "Well, thank you, but I believe I'll stay in the church across the street- and please don't mention my presence here or there to anyone."

The man's eyes widen. "B-b-but they're *Protestants!* Worse- they're *Baptists.*"

"I'm sure my soul will survive the night, Sir."

He nods shakily. "I will pray for you."

I raise my eyebrows. "Uh, thank you." I suppose my soul does need all the help it can get.

The sun gets steadily lower on the horizon, so I make my way across the street, shaking like the old man was. Ridiculous, really; I'm sure I won't be attacked by the wolf the *moment* night falls.

I cringe. I will no doubt need the wolf's assistance again tomorrow unless I decide to accept Amos' help instead. If only there was a way to find Thomas without accepting *either* of their help...

I suppose I could follow Amos without his knowledge- he is going to the same place as I, after all- but I probably wouldn't be able to keep it from his knowledge for long.

My eyes fall on a shop next to the church, its window displaying dresses and hats. I smile. That might do nicely.

~~~

I dash from the shop to the church, my heart thundering in my chest. Why does shopping take so long? Why?

Somehow, I manage to live long enough to make it inside the church.

Now shaking even worse than the old priest, I curl up on a pew. Then I attempt to follow his example further and pray for myself, but I can't seem to make my mind focus. The memory of the wolf's voice in my head haunts me.

I guess that's what I get for letting my mind stay connected to his for so long. I will not be making the same mistake again.

I glance down at my purchases. These had better work...

Then I glance up at the church walls around me. Those had better work too. I sure hope this being a Baptist church won't lessen the sacredness of the ground...

Chapter Ten
In which I wear a dress and spend the day staring at Amos

I gape at the lovely girl staring back at me from the bathroom mirror. With my hair secured on the top of my head and a hat over it; a dark blue dress replacing my overalls- the most elegant one I could find too- and makeup on my face for the first time ever, I finally look and feel stylish. Too bad I can't let Amos see me like this.

I put some more rouge under my eyes in attempt to conceal the dark bags. The sun hasn't even risen yet, and I feel strongly attracted to the pew that was so uncomfortable last night. If the wolf starts singing lullabies to me right now, I think I might just fall asleep standing.

Focus, Jane. I need to stay awake and wait for Amos- he'll no doubt exit the cathedral at the break of dawn. He's just like Father in that way: working himself to death. Men of vision and calling often forget about their own limitations in their zeal.

I sigh. Father wasn't always so intense; he was much more balanced when Mother lived with us... Then again, that was before I was scarred. Is it *my* fault that Mother left- and that Father worked himself nearly to death?

I shake my head. No. It was the wolf's fault. Oh, he is going to *pay*. As for Amos, I really do hope he finds his cousin again- as well as a nice girl to balance his personality. Obviously, that girl couldn't be me; one who hunts werewolves and one hunted by a werewolf together? Ridiculous.

Actually, though, come to think of it, it makes perfect sense...

Across the street, Amos himself emerges from the cathedral as I knew he would.

Thoughts scattering to the wind, I focus on my premeditated steps. I pick up my backpack and, once Amos has disappeared from view, I also step outside. Once I spot Amos again, thankfully walking with his back to me, I realize that I have no idea how to properly stalk someone. Obviously, the vigorous education Father gave me on has holes. Really, how could he have taught me how to track animals but not how to stalk people?

I wonder how Father is faring at the moment...

Amos disappears down another street. I snap out of my musing, straighten my bonnet, and follow him.

The new street is almost entirely vacant besides us, with just a few stragglers, most of whom appear to have just transformed from being werewolves, here and there. I frown; I was hoping for a crowd to hide in- and not a crowd that looks as grumpy as this one.

Amos keeps walking forward and I keep following him, silently praying that he doesn't turn around- and that none of the potential werewolves grab me or something.

Suddenly, people begin stepping out of their homes and heading to work, and I realize that the sun is all the way up now. Good little pastoral village comprised of early birds.

Amos glances back and I pretend to be talking to a housewife. When he turns back around, I wait several moments before continuing to follow him.

Good morning, my pet.

"Go away," I mutter. "I don't need you."

Oh, I think you do.

I imagine a silver cross and, just like that, he's gone. Why didn't I think of that before?

In my preoccupation, my foot catches the hem of my new skirt and sends me flying several feet forward, into Amos. I jump up and dive behind a nearby milk cart. Through an empty milk bottle, I watch as Amos glances around before shrugging and continuing onward.

I remain where I am for a moment longer to wait for my heart to quiet down. What an unfortunate hole in my education I have found. And what a long, long day I have ahead of me...

Amos reaches the edge of the village, and without a moment's hesitation, he plunges right into a forest. I, however, pause.

I didn't follow the wolf into the forest, but this is Amos. There is a huge difference between the two. One would hurt me and the other would protect me... Though he's not above hurting me to protect me.

Amos disappears from view. Taking a deep breath, I plunge into the forest after him.

Unlike the quaint pastoral village, this place smells of potential danger, but also unlike the village, this is my element. And, true, the forest where I grew up had a werewolf problem, but it also housed the beautiful stag. So often the world and the things within it can be used either for good or for evil, and it's up to us to use discretion when using them. As Father is always saying, we must be as wise as serpents but as innocent as doves.

Since I know all about tracking through forests, I allow

the distance between Amos and me to increase and try to follow his tracks. However, he proves to be very good at covering his tracks, so I have to hurry and catch up to him enough so that I can see him with my own eyes.

Suddenly, a snake, probably summoned by my musings on his wisdom, slithers onto my path and I accidentally release a yelp. Then I jump behind a tree before Amos can look back and see me.

Heart thumping, I attempt to listen for Amos over my overly noisy organ.

And I hear twigs snapping as someone approaches me.

Silently as I can despite my loud heart, I grab the closest branch above me and pull myself up. Then I climb up another and another before pressing myself against the trunk just as Amos rounds the tree.

I watch as he studies the ground I was standing on and then the area around it. Biting my lip, I wait for him to look up.

He never does.

Shaking his head, Amos goes back around the tree and continues on his way.

I release my breath and count to one hundred before climbing down and following him again. This time, though, I decide to go back to tracking him. Thankfully, he proves to be much easier this time, and I'm able to follow him outside the forest to a surprisingly large city.

"Follow that carriage please," I tell my newest cabbie- I've become quite the cab patron- gesturing to the cab Amos is hiring.

"You mean like a real, actual cab chase?" he asks.

"I've always wanted to do one of them."

"Be discreet," I order.

"Of course, ma'am; I'll be nothing but."

When my cab swerves around a pedestrian making me feel as though the entire cab is destined to go flying into the nearest building- and not for the first time, either- I begin to wonder what it was the cabbie promised to be 'nothing but.'

After a long trip that seemed longer with death trying to hitch a ride, Amos' cab finally comes to a halt. Mine comes to a halt too, though a little behind his (very little- for a moment there I was convinced that we were going to ram right *into* Amos' cab).

"Get your own carriage, Death," I mutter as I climb out of the cab. While I pay my cabbie and come to the decision to take some other means of transport next time, I take in my surroundings.

The first thing I notice is how dark it is outside, and how late it must be. The second thing I notice is that I appear to be at some sort of bloated dinner party with more people bustling around than I realized the world even contained.

Wow; I must have really misjudged Amos' workaholicness.

The third thing I notice is that Amos is still wearing his green garb which, good as he looks in it, is not fit for a dinner party. The grim expression he wears on his face is equally unfit.

Suddenly, I become aware of a fourth thing: my scar has a slight buzzing feeling I haven't felt for a long time, if ever. Something strange is happening at this party- well, besides the ridiculous dances and flirtations anyway.

    I remove my new silver dagger from my back pack and slide it up my sleeve, sending shivers throughout my body. Then I secure the sheathe there before pulling down my sleeve, straightening my bonnet, and making my way to my first party.

Chapter Eleven

In which I crash a party, dance with strange men, and meet another kind of monster

I make my way through the crowd, not sure of my destination. Suddenly, I'm intercepted by a gentleman.

"I don't believe we've met," he says. "We'll have to change that."

Next thing I know, I'm being twirled on the dance floor amongst hundreds of other couples.

"Now tell me," my dance partner says. "Who are you?"

"That is none of your business, sir," I answer, trying to figure out what I feel about this sudden development; hard to tell between the dizzying dance steps I can't seem to keep up with and his close proximity that I can't seem to avoid.

"Ah, but it's my business to know the name of every baby vamp I come across," he counters.

I blink. I *really* don't know what to think now. And why does *he* think that I'm an infant vampire? And thinking that, why does he want to dance with me?

"You don't have to talk," he adds. "There are other things we can do with our mouths."

I bite my tongue and try to think of something to say. "Well, we can breathe and whistle- oh, and eat." My eyes go to the large refreshments table bordering the dance floor where Amos is sipping punch.

I open my mouth to excuse myself from the dance, but I'm interrupted by a silky voice stealing my words. "Excuse me."

My partner and I turn to see a tall handsome, if pale, man next to us.

"I'm afraid I must cut in," the newer stranger adds.

"I'm afraid you *can't*," my partner counters.

"Is that so?"

I use his distraction to pull away from my partner and make my way to the refreshments table, making sure to keep my distance from Amos. I'll keep him in view, but I don't need to be in *his* view to do so. I'm not risking a silver bracelet from him *ever* again.

Someone pours me a glass of punch which I sip. Then I quickly put it down. That is most definitely *not* punch.

"I don't believe we've met, Jane," someone says behind me.

I turn around and find a woman with hair so short that even in a crowd of bobbed women, she looks boyish at first glance. "If we've never met, how do you know my name?"

"Oh, it's Jane? See, that's just what I call all women. Like you call men Charlie."

"I... don't."

"Oh." She looks me up and down like I'm some kind of novelty. "Well, I'm Daisy."

"Jane," I offer.

She nods and takes a glass of Not Punch. "Parties like this can get a little crazy."

I nod back, not sure what to say, if anything.

Another woman approaches. I can't tell much about her except that she's wearing more makeup than I've ever seen on a single individual at one time before. "Hi, Daisy," she says. "And who's this?"

"Jane," Daisy answers.

"That's quite a kneeduster, Jane," the new arrival says. "Very plain. Plain Jain. How quaint."

I look down at the dusky blue gown that doesn't seem to fit next to my two companions' sequined dresses.

"It is quite old-fashioned," Daisy agrees.

Her friend chortles. "I was going for rustic."

"*Lu*," Daisy scolds lightheartedly.

"What?" Lu asks. "That seemed like a nicer term than 'hideously passé.'" She chortles again.

Daisy slips into laughter with her.

"At least I'm not ashamed of my face," I retort.

Daisy keeps laughing. "She's as sharp as Jordan!"

Lu, however, doesn't seem to think so and stops laughing abruptly. Before she can react, though, my ex-partner approaches us.

"Hello again, beautiful," he says.

I open my mouth to tell him that he can take his flattery somewhere else, but then I find that he has. In fact, he seems to be flirting with both Daisy and Lu at once.

I roll my eyes and walk away, passing several loud conversations on the way.

"Hot dawg!" one young man yelps, thumping another on the shoulder, and I turn to stare at them as I walk to make sure he's not actually assaulting him.

Then, I'm distracted by another man to my right, saying in a low voice, "I have to go see a man about a dog."

Maybe he should talk to the guy with the overly warm canine-

"Hello, Miss," Amos says, suddenly beside me, a glass in his hand.

I stiffen. How did I forget about him?

"I don't believe we've met," he adds, putting his glass down.

Is he being sarcastic? Or does he really not recognize me with my hair up?

Wordlessly, Amos pulls me onto the dance floor.

He must recognize me; Amos doesn't seem like a cake-eater. Then again, I didn't think he was the kind of guy who'd put silver on a girl with lycanthropy.

I know so little of the savage race known as man.

"So, the weather is balmy tonight," Amos says as he leads me through a dance I don't know (not that I know *any* dances- another hole in my education).

"Quite," I agree. What is his game? I have to stall until I can figure it out. "What are you doing in this part of the country?"

"Business."

Business. Right. *That's* why he's dancing with me. "Are you having fun?"

"At this particular moment, yes."

Does that mean he knows it's me or not? "Do you know anyone here?"

"A few notables." He glances past me and surveys our surroundings.

What does he mean? Why is everything he says so cryptic?! It's time for the ultimate test. "I'm sorry, but I don't believe I caught your name."

He smiles wryly. "Amos. Amos Hood. Yours?"

"Katherine." Well, it's my middle name anyway.

His smile doesn't shift. "Ah, I should have known. You look like a Katherine."

Does that mean he doesn't recognize me? Or is he just playing along? I need to get myself another ultimate test.

Amos scans the crowd again. He appears to focus on something and his jaw clenches.

I glance back and notice the pale man who had tried to intercept my first dance, talking to a familiar young woman.

Debra.

Amos pulls me closer to himself and begins propelling us both through the crowd. The more ground we cover the more he picks up his pace until we're practically running.

Neither the pale man nor Debra seem to notice our approach as they're quite caught up in each other. The pale man whispers something into Debra's ear and she nods. Then they both disappear into a dark corner.

"He'd better not hurt her," Amos mutters, about to dive into the darkness after them. Then he notices my hand in his and frowns. "Can I trust you to stay here, Jane?"

I frown. He's known it's me all along. Or he's just using slang. Applesauce- even the English *language* has turned against me. "No. And don't attempt to tie me down with silver again either."

"I really am sorry about that. I wasn't thinking rationally at the time; I was desperate- like I am now. Please forgive me." He plunges us both into the darkness.

When my eyes become adjusted, I find that it's not so

much a corner as it is a large unlit area. A few scattered couples and individuals inhabit the darkness, apparently necking it, but Amos pulls us towards one couple in particular.

"You're even lovelier in the moonlight," the pale man whispers to Debra as he pushes her hair away from her neck

I feel strangely flattered, even though he's talking to Debra. How can I be not be affected by someone with such a beautiful voice?

My scar aches suddenly, snapping me into focus.

The man glances up. "Who's there?" His gaze falls on Amos, who has unsheathed his sword and then to me. The man frowns and pushes a startled Debra at Amos, who drops his sword to catch her. Then the man grabs me and pulls me to himself.

Amos quickly drops Debra and picks up his sword again, which he aims at the pale man holding me.

"Don't move or else I bite her," the pale man hisses at Amos. Then he lowers his eyes to my neck. "Though, I may not be able to resist her for much longer..."

"Release her, vampire," Amos orders. "And I may yet show you mercy."

The vampire laughs. "It is I who am in the position to show mercy, not you. Unfortunately, I am not in a merciful mood."

Amos lunges, but the vampire wraps his cloak around him and myself. Then he moves to bite my throat.

Great; as if lycanthropy isn't bad enough.

Suddenly, I'm being thrown to the ground. From my new perspective, I watch as the vampire staggers backwards, retching as if he's smelled something horrid.

"She's been claimed by a *wolf*!" he cries. "A *wolf*! Wretched, *disgusting* wench."

I've disgusted a vampire. And now I'm indebted to the wolf. This just is not my day.

"Allow me to put you out of your misery, monster!" Amos cries, lunging at the vampire.

A moment later, Amos is helping me up. "Are you all right?" he asks. Without waiting for an answer, he brushes his fingers along my neck. "It's a miracle: you're clean- no bite-marks."

I touch my scar. "I think I know why."

"Why'd you do that?!" Debra cries suddenly.

"Excuse me?" Amos asks, turning to her.

"I almost had him!" Debra answers. She holds up a dagger that, by the way it sends a shiver down my spine, I assume must be laden with silver. The Hoods are just dripping with silver weapons.

"You're not supposed to be here at all," Amos snaps.

"I refuse to spend my life as a Rapunzel, Cousin."

I back away slowly to give them room to bicker and me room to escape, but Amos grabs my wrist- he seems to have a thing for wrists.

"You're staying with us," Amos tells me.

"There is no 'us,'" Debra retorts.

Amos grabs her wrist too.

"Let me go!" we both cry in unison.

"You are both coming back with me," he answers.

"I'm going to find my brother!" I counter.

"I'm going to help!" Debra adds.

"I'll go search for him myself once you two are safe,"

Amos answers.

I glance at the crumpled body of the probably deceased vampire. A werewolf would no doubt see the same fate from Amos.

Not my brother.

Moving my free arm to the one grasped by Amos, I remove the dagger from my sleeve and hold it up to Amos' neck. "You will let me rescue my brother."

Amos mutters something and turns to his cousin.

"Don't look at me," she mutters back. "Unlike you, *I* stay out of other people's fights."

Amos mutters again before turning back to me. "Now, Miss, I don't believe you're that kind of girl."

"Not usually," I agree, pressing the dagger a little closer to Amos' neck. "But I'm desperate."

Amos closes his eyes for a moment. Then he releases my hand.

I back away slowly, still pointing my dagger at him. However, Amos remains where he is, so I turn around and take off running.

But I'm not running alone.

I turn to see Amos and Debra running towards me.

"What do you think you're doing?" I demand.

"Coming with you," Amos answers, not missing a step. "If I can't stop you, then I'm forced to help you. And if you are the genius you claim to be, you won't refuse my assistance."

I mentally weigh the pros and cons. Then I slow my pace. "I will not hesitate to hurt you if you try to thwart my mission."

"I don't doubt it, Miss."

"I'll help you keep him in line," Debra assures.

Amos gives her look that is both exasperated and amused.

"We have an understanding then," I say. Then, together with Amos and Debra, I put distance between myself and the party and focus on something much more commendable.

I will find you, Thomas. Whatever it takes.

Chapter Twelve
In which I put up with the Hoods, am put up with by the Hoods, and see New York City for the first time

Where are you, my pet?

Something grabs my shoulders, and I throw myself at it, causing us both to fall with a hard thud. I wake up and find myself on top of a startled Amos.

"I thought I made it clear that I am your ally," Amos says dryly. "And I was just trying to wake you."

"I thought you were the wolf," I explain, attempting to stand up and succeeding in accidentally kneeing Amos in the gut.

Amos cringes. "I am comforted, then, with the knowledge that, should the wolf ever come upon you, you will not be completely helpless."

"You should know that you two have utterly scandalized the pastor of this hospitable church," Debra says, standing over us and securing the red cloak around her shoulders.

"That's a beautiful cloak," I breathe, finally righting myself. "Where *did* you get it?"

"Should I hire a cab for us?" Debra asks Amos, pointedly ignoring me.

Why are these Hoods so secretive about their clothing?

Amos nods. "And I'll go buy us some breakfast."

Moments later, the three of us are, I'm afraid, in a cab. My only comfort is eating the hot cross buns Amos bought for us.

"When we get to the city, will we stay at a hotel or in

another church?" Debra asks.

I cringe at the thought of sleeping on another pew.

"If you want to sleep in a nice feather bed, you should have stayed at home, Debra," Amos answers.

"I want to help more than I want a feather bed," Debra retorts. "Above all I want to see the world; to do *something* with my life."

I glance down at my bread. How many times had I asked Father to let me see the world? Now I know why he wouldn't let me: the wolf would have exacted its vengeance... Like it did on that poor innocent town.

I was merely expressing my displeasure.

I tense up and glance at the cousins, who are both glaring at each other and ignoring me. Then I turn away and whisper, "Did you... did you kill anyone?" I dread the answer, but I dread not knowing as well.

Not that night. Rest assured that I've only had to kill two creatures in my life and neither of them were mortal.

Does that mean Uncle Vincent wasn't mortal? "'Only' two? Do you think that earns you a medal or something, wolf?"

Compared to other werewolves, it is an incredible feat. I was blessed with a higher hunger than mere flesh, as shall you when you become like me.

"And what higher hunger would that be, murderer?"

You shall soon see, my pet.

"Just tell me!" I demand, but I get no answer from the wolf and only a weird look from Debra.

"You know as well as I that it is dangerous for us out here," Amos tells Debra, completely oblivious to me and the conversation I just had. "Do you not remember the vampire?"

"Which I had under control," she answers. "And why, cousin, when it's probably more dangerous out here for you, are you still allowed out and not I?"

"It's different for me."

"Why? Because you're a *boy*?"

"No, it's not that exactly. I'm trained."

"What about all those hours I poured into study and preparation for fighting monsters? Doesn't that count for anything?"

"There are other factors that you aren't aware of, cousin."

"Well there are some factors that *you* aren't aware of, *cousin*."

Amos groans. "Why are you even arguing with me about this? It was my father's decision; not mine."

"But you agree with it."

"My acquiescence makes no difference in the matter. What is it you want from this argument?"

She looks him in the eyes. "Tell me why it's different for me."

Amos sighs. "My parents weren't murdered."

I freeze, waiting for Debra to cry or yell or do something else dramatic, but she just nods. Then she turns to me. "Your father was wrong about ghosts; they do exist in the fact that the dead's decisions haunt the living."

Amos groans and turns to me. "You've been awfully silent, Jane. Are you angry with me too?"

I shake my head. "I certainly don't have any reason to be... Except that the last time I trusted you, you tied me down like a dog with a silver bracelet."

"You know, most girls appreciate getting jewelry."

I glare at him. "I'm not most girls, and you know it. You manipulated my lycanthropy for your own purposes."

"My own purposes being to protect you while I searched for my cousin."

Debra sniffs.

"What a great job you did protecting me," I agree. "With the bane of wolves."

"You know, you didn't seem so against silver when you pressed *my* silver knife against *my* neck," he points out.

"I was going off to fight a werewolf. I needed a weapon, even if it pained me to take it... Though it was worth it to get to use it on you."

Amos shakes his head.

The cab jolts to a stop.

Amos frowns. "We're not in New York yet."

"The wheels are stuck in mud," our cabbie announces. "Everyone out; I'm going to need to push her."

We all climb out and while the cabbie puts his back against the cab and pushes. When it becomes obvious that if we waited on the cabbie we would be there for a while, Amos steps forward to help.

I try not to watch as Amos rolls up his sleeves, revealing the fruits of wielding a silver sword, but I find it almost impossible not to. Every time I glance away, my eyes drift back on their own accord.

Thinking of me, pet?

"Go away," I mutter.

Debra glances at me and I force a smile. She shrugs and glances back to the road.

I can show you your brother again.

I freeze.

Not so quick to be done with me when you know I can give you what you want, are you?

"Show him to me," I order.

Close your eyes.

I do, and suddenly I see Thomas walking to a dock. He pauses and speaks with a distinguished-looking man wearing a captain's uniform. Thomas hands him a pouch of money.

"He's leaving," I whisper.

Yes. You must hurry, my pet.

I open my eyes and find that the cabbie and Amos have made some progress, but not enough. Rolling up my own sleeves, I march over and begin pushing alongside the boys. My extra effort proves to be all the cab needs, because it lurches forward suddenly, and I go forward with it.

Before I can take a face plant in the mud, Amos grabs me by the elbow and pulls me up.

"Thank you," I gasp.

"Can't have you getting your nice dress muddy just because you're doing dirty work," Amos says dryly.

I nod in agreement- wait, was he being sarcastic?

"Come on," Amos adds, opening the cab door for Debra and me. "I need to get you ladies to the city before dark."

~~~

I gape at the city outside the cab window. Just last week I was reentering civilization; now I'm in *New York*.

"First time in the big apple?" Amos asks.

I nod eagerly. Then I blush when I realize what a country bumpkin I must seem like.

"Mine too," adds Debra, who has been silent since her argument with Amos.

Amos glances at her before whispering something to the cabbie. A moment later, the cabbie pulls up at a luxurious-looking restaurant.

"Ladies," Amos announces with an elegant bow.

I go back to looking like a country bumpkin. "I wish I could just naturally turn on the Ritz."

"There's no such thing," Debra says.

Our cabbie opens the cab door for us and then Amos opens the restaurant door for us. The restaurant is crowded, with dim lighting, a hazy atmosphere due to smoke, and a singer on a stage wearing a flashy dress and singing so softly that her voice is just a background sound against the smatterings of conversation. I'm not sure what to say, so I say nothing and strike my most elegant pose.

"Table for three, please," Amos tells a waitress, who somehow finds us just such a table despite the crowd.

I study the menu she hands us. "What should I order?"

"Anything you want," Amos answers. "It's your first time in New York, after all. Don't worry; it's on me."

I choose the cheapest meat dish on the menu. Debra chooses the most expensive.

"Do you feel better now?" Amos asks her.

"Yes."

"Then why do you still look so sullen?"

"I'm not sullen; just thinking."

"Oh, no," Amos mutters good-naturally.

"What are you thinking about, Debra?" I ask.

"What your father said about ghosts."

Amos cringes.

"And?" I ask.

"Ghosts are people's desire to be reunited with loved ones and know what the afterlife holds, right? Well, I think all recurring legends are sort of like that. Sure, we know vampires, werewolves, faerie folk exist, and merfolk- more or less- exist, but even if they didn't, I think we'd still have legends about them."

"How so?" I ask eagerly. I do love a good theory. Thomas used to insist that we had strong Athenian blood in us, and while he got the love of beauty, I got the love of knowledge.

Oh, Thomas...

"We, as humans are generally discontent with our lives," Debra answers. "We know we were meant for more, but as most of us do not know how to become more, we invent things that *are* more to make our drab lives more interesting."

Amos laughs dryly. "So you're saying that even if I didn't know they were real, I would be so much more content to imagine bloodthirsty vampires and raging werewolves are real than if I didn't?"

"Sometimes it's easier to imagine monsters than to face real ones," Debra counters. "Besides, I hear merfolk are good for marrying and faeries for granting wishes."

"I know, Red," Amos answers. "I was just teasing."

"Sorry if I was defensive, Robin, but it's hard to know whether you are being serious or not with that dry humor of yours."

"Red?" I ask. "Robin? That sounds like a restaurant or something."

"Our nicknames for each other," Amos explains. "We're both Hoods, and because she loves that red cloak of hers, she's Little Red Riding Hood."

"And he's Robin Hood," Debra adds. "Because he's all about 'kill the strong to protect the weak.'"

I giggle, but Amos frowns. "I do not 'kill' anyone," he counters. "I slay monsters. And if they were human once, they are no longer."

I subconsciously reach up to touch my scar. Does Amos see me as half monster? Half animal?

Debra narrows her eyes at Amos and then nods towards me.

Amos follows her gaze before adding quickly, "*You're* not a monster, Miss. The creature that did this to you is, though."

"And if I turn?" I whisper.

"I won't let it happen."

"But if it does? And what about my brother? What if he's turned?"

Before Amos can answer, Debra laughs- laughs! "My, Robin, you certainly have a way with the ladies. And after all your boasting, too."

I raise my eyebrows, trying to hide my disappointment over my unanswered question with amusement.

"I do in fact have a 'way with the ladies,'" Amos counters with mock haughtiness. "I'm quite the big timer."

I raise my eyebrows higher. "Is that so?"

"Show her your method," Debra urges.

"Yes, do," I agree.

"Okay," he says, "but you've brought this upon yourself." He nudges me slightly and then gives me an expression of mock shock. "Oh, I'm sorry, Miss; I didn't see you there. Though, how I could have missed you is beyond me." He scrutinizes my face, suddenly all pretense gone. "Wow, your eyes..."

I stare back at him with the eyes that seem to be my best attribute, taking in his face which is not lacking in good attributes itself.

Debra laughs, breaking our trance and leaving me feeling embarrassed and vulnerable. "I can't believe I didn't realize earlier that you were just kidding about your method being so effective!" she cries.

"I wasn't!" Amos exclaims.

"But it's so *corny.*"

"Jane can be the judge of that," Amos says turning to me. "What do *you* think of my method?"

It makes me feel all jittery inside. "It needs to be updated."

Amos pretends to be wounded.

Debra laughs. "How the mighty have fallen. Really, you Delanes have opened my eyes to Amos' tomfoolery."

"I didn't fall," he counters. "I was ruthlessly dragged down."

I smile. They remind me of Thomas and me.

Sadness hits me and I cling to Thomas's memory and don't let go.

~~~

"As requested," Amos says, gesturing to an elegant hotel room.

"Are you sure it's safe?" I ask nervously, searching the room with my eyes like the wolf might suddenly jump out at us.

Amos inspects the window and one of the two doors. "I've slept in less secure places."

Debra throws herself onto one of the beds before sitting up again. "Wait; there are only two beds."

"I'll be sleeping in the adjoining room," Amos answers, gesturing to the door he hadn't checked.

I frown. I'm really beginning to doubt the security of the plan.

"You mean you're not going mother hen on us?" Debra asks.

"Do you want me to?"

"No!"

"That's what I thought." Amos removes his hat and hands it to me. "Don't ask any questions; just put this on and don't take it off until morning. Understand?"

His tone is so serious that I nod and immediately place the hat on my head. Not even Debra scoffs.

Amos nods approvingly. Then he says, "Good night, ladies," before leaving the room.

I touch the strange hat on my head and wonder how,

despite my not sleeping in a church, I feel very, very safe. And smile because while Amos may not be in the same room with us, his hat makes him feel very, very close.

Chapter Thirteen
In which I face both a nightmare and a broken dream

"So..." I begin as I settle into my bed.

Debra ignores me and settles into her own bed.

"You don't have to answer or anything," I add. "But I have a question."

"Hmm?"

"How did... how did you survive when the werewolf attacked your family?"

Debra studies me from across the room. "Why do you want to know?"

I bite my lip, already regretting voicing my question. "Well, it seems like something I ought to know since I'm kind of being hunted by a werewolf..."

"Uh-huh." She rolls over and studies the ceiling. "Well, I heard the wolf break down the door and my mother screaming, so I ran into my parents' room just as my father ran out of it."

Surprised that she's actually telling me the story, I move to the edge of my bed so that I can hear her better.

"I was scared to be alone, but even more scared to follow my father to the source of my mother's scream," Her voice is calm and detached, but I can hear the scars of great grief and fear. "And, you see, my father was always a very messy person, with his dirty clothing constantly scattered all over the floor. Mother used to get so angry with him about it..."

I can't help but wonder what that has to do with the werewolf, but I don't voice my question lest it make Debra change her mind about telling her story.

"Anyway, I hid under his old cloak because it smelled of him and I found that very comforting. Then I heard something enter their room."

Breath leaves my lungs in anticipation- or, for it, retreat.

"I could sense its evil and remained very still, hoping it wouldn't sense me."

If I wasn't breathless then, I'd be now.

"Obviously, it didn't. Father's musk masked my smell and saved my life."

"Is that your father's cloak?" I ask, nodding towards her red cloak draped over the end of her bed.

"No. My father's cloak was burned at his memorial service in place of his body, which was never found."

"Oh." I fight the urge to be sick. "I'm so sorry. Was... was the wolf ever killed?" It couldn't be my wolf, could it? He claimed to have never slain mortals....

"My uncle hunted it down and battled it, but that werewolf was stronger than he expected," Debra answers. "It escaped half-dead, and Uncle Arthur tracked it down until he came across the werewolf's body in a mountainous region. We don't know if it died of its wounds or if someone finished him off, but either way, the monster is dead. That was eleven years ago."

I nod and lean back onto my bed, feeling sad for Debra and her loss. And, for the strangest reason, I also feel sad for the wolf- not the one who murdered Debra's parents, but the one who is hunting me even now.

~~~

Guten tag, my pet.

My eyes fly open and I find the wolf above me, its yellow yes looking down at me and its mouth curled into something of a smile.

Before I can scream, it lunges at me. However, its teeth do not penetrate my skin. The wolf is puzzled by this- as am I. However, I am encouraged enough to scream.

Amos comes running into the room, his sword drawn. The moment he sees the wolf, he lunges at it and stabs the wolf in the side. My own side burns for some reason and I shriek with pain.

The wolf howls and throws itself at Amos, knocking the hunter into the wall. My would-be rescuer slumps over and doesn't get back up.

I scream again.

Debra comes rushing out of nowhere, picks up Amos' sword, and stands between him and the monster that has invaded our bedchamber. The wolf stares at her, sniffs, takes a faltering step backwards, and then jumps out of the broken window. Debra drops the sword and falls to her knees, shaking.

I climb out of bed and hurry to Amos where I press my fingers to his neck. When I find his pulse, I release a breath I didn't realize I had been holding. Then I turn to Debra. "We need to get him to the hospital."

"We have to wait until morning," Debra answers shakily. "The wolf- "

"Is injured and won't dare to attack again," I finish.

"How do you know?"

"I just do." I definitely wouldn't attack again with my

side burning the way it is. "Stay with Amos until I get help."

Debra nods, her eyes wide with terror.

As I hurry out of the room, I mentally scold Debra for wanting a hotel room, Amos for obliging, and me for acquiescing. Sure, wanting to sleep in a bed instead of a pew is innocent enough, but it wasn't wise. Father *said* we must be innocent as doves but as wise as serpents.

And nothing of wolves. In fact, innocence and wisdom is the only way for sheep to survive in a world of wolves.

In my hurry, I run into a young man walking up the hallway, startling us both. "I need help," I blurt. "My friend's been injured."

"Have you called the hospital?" the man asks in a rather rhythmical voice with a slight accent.

I shake my head. "Not yet; I haven't found a phone."

"I know where one is," he assures. "I'll go make the call."

I lean wearily against the wall. "Thank you."

He nods and hurries off with a slight limp. I wait for a moment until my breath catches up with me and then follow him to the hotel counter where I watch as he makes his call.

"An ambulance is on its way," he announces when he's done.

"Thank you again," I breathe.

"I'm also a medical student," he adds. "I might be able to help more-"

I drag him to Amos before he can finish his own sentence. As he looks over Amos, I pace.

"Thank you," Debra tells him. "What's your name?"

I cringe for not thinking to ask that much earlier. My father really failed in teaching us our manners.

"Dwayne," the man answers. "Dwayne Fisher."

"Thank you ever so much, Mr. Fisher," I say. "We are *indebted* to you."

"Think nothing of it. And please, call me Dwayne."

"Dwayne," I repeat, studying the young man. His hair is blonde and his face is almost babyish, like he is still very young, but in a somehow charming sort of way. His eyes are the color of the sea.

The ambulance comes quickly, and Debra and I find ourselves in Amos' hospital room before I have even had time to register a transition.

"He's stable," the nurse tells us, "and I have the utmost confidence he will wake shortly."

I nod and go to the window. It's a relief to see the sun- but it's higher than I had expected. The last few hours have passed in such a blur... Has Thomas left already?

Frantically, my eyes scan the crowd below, even though I know my chances of spotting my brother amongst so many people are slim to none.

My eyes focus on a lone figure walking at the fringe of the crowd, and I know with all certainty that I am looking at my long-lost brother. Just as I know with the same certainty that it wasn't with a human skill that I found him.

I push away such thoughts and focus on what is before me, but when I turn around to claim it, I remember that I'm in a hospital room.

"Debra!" I cry. "My brother- I've spotted him!"

"Then go!" she urges. "I can watch my cousin."

I nod and move to remove my hat, but Debra shakes her head.

"I don't know what that hat is capable of," she says, "but I do know that Amos would want you to have it since he cannot presently protect you himself."

"Thank you," I blurt before taking off as fast as I dare in a hospital.

By the time I escape the building and have push through the crowd, Thomas is no longer where I had seen him. But there's no need to panic; as incomplete as my education is, I *do* know how to track a man.

I know how to sense one as well, apparently, for it isn't so much the physical traces of my brother I follow but the smells and feelings he left behind. I didn't know I could do that before. My brother has never been so emotional before either. Also, it's rather obvious that he's been living near fish for too long.

Finally, I come upon Thomas as he unlocks the door of a cabin smaller than our shed back home. It appears to be ready to fly into the bay at the next gust of wind- or gust from a wolf. As it is, the bay is so near one would think it had slithered up the shore when it grew impatient with the wind to feed it the cabin.

I grin at my long-lost relation and suddenly feel giddier and happier than I've been in a long time. My brother is alive and he's right here. "Thomas!" I cry, throwing my arms around him.

Thomas pulls away and whips around so fast that his hood flies off (but not into the hungry bay, much to the water's disappointment), revealing his sallow face accented by dark bags under desperate eyes and hair shaggier than I've ever seen it (and it can get really shaggy before he lets me come near his head with scissors).

"Thomas, it's me," I add, suddenly uncertain. The boy standing before me is Thomas, but not as I expected to find him. "I'm your sister Jane... remember?"

Thomas closes his eyes like my voice pains him. Then my gentle brother, who never before in his life raised his voice, snaps, "Be gone, fool girl." With that, he hurries into his cabin, slamming the door shut between us.

~~~

I don't move from the building my brother disappeared into; he'll have to depart from his shack sooner or later. He will not scare me away so easily. I refuse to give up on my hunt when I know he's right here.

Nightfall brings with it a cool breeze from the sea. However, it's not the cold wind that sends chills down my spine.

Huddling against the shack, I hope and pray that the wolf is too wounded to hunt this night, or at least that the smell of fish covers my scent. It's no comfort to me that my side feels perfectly recovered. To my relief, though, I hear no howls.

I do, however, hear whistles.

Looking up, I find several boys at the brink of manhood approaching me.

"I wouldn't sleep there if I were you, little girl," one

boy says. "They say a monster in man's form lives there."

"No monster abides her," I answer coolly. Thomas could never deserve that title.

"A madman then," another boy says.

"Come with us if you're smart," a third boy adds.

"I am smart," I say. "So I'll remain right here, thank you very much."

"Now, don't be silly," they chide.

The door behind me bursts open, and Thomas appears, holding a chair. He tosses it at the boys, who scatter.

"Stay away from my sister," he growls.

The boys don't need to be told twice.

Thomas watches them flee until they are out of sight. Then he turns to me. "I told you to go."

"It's a good thing you're not my father, then," I answer, standing up. "I don't have to listen to you."

Thomas scowls. Then he grabs me by my arm and drags me into the shack.

I pull away from him once we're inside and take in the one room- if you could call it that- which contains simply a bed, a table, and one chair until Thomas retrieves the other. When he shuts the door behind him, he sniffs the air like he smells something terrible, which isn't surprising since this hut is saturated with the smell of fish. Still, I don't think that's it.

I glance at my sleeve concealing my dagger and tell myself that he can't be smelling that. After all, simple logic says you can't smell silver.

But it can call to you...

Glaring at me, Thomas drops onto one of the chairs

with all the attitude of an exclamation point before gesturing to the bed. "Since you're stuck here for the night, you might as well get some sleep."

I decide to listen to him this time. "Good night then, Thomas. I love you."

Despite the dim light, I can still see the heartbroken expression on Thomas's face until he brings his hands up to hide it.

Chapter Fourteen
In which I both learn of and face surprises

When I wake up, I find Thomas sitting at the table, his back straight and a napkin on his lap. Two places have been set, both with plates filled with meaty breakfast pastries.

Mm, meat.

I quickly go to the other chair and sit down.

"Would you like to say grace, Jane?" Thomas asks in his usual thoughtful manner. Something about him seems gentler than last night, more like the brother I came to find.

"Very well," I agree, noticing that his pastries have been untouched- he's been waiting for me. It's a relief to know that no matter what, Thomas's table manners will remain impeccable.

After I've prayed, Thomas cuts a pastry in half and puts part of it in his mouth. When he swallows that a second later, the other half joins it. Once his mouth is clear again, he says around the napkin wiping his mouth, "I'm glad to see you again, Jane, but you have to return home. It's not safe to be around me."

"You'd never hurt me," I assure, ignoring what he must be hinting at. "Besides, it's not safe for me to be alone, thanks to the wolf."

Thomas puts down the pastry he was about to eat. "The wolf is dead. I killed it."

"I'm afraid that the wolf is still very much alive."

Thomas frowns. "But I shot it with a silver bullet; I saw it transform into a man and stumble away, bleeding."

I frown back. There were only two trails of footprints, though: one man and one wolf. Now logic drops a hint of its own, but I ignore it like I ignored Thomas'. "You might have injured him, but you didn't kill him. He's attacked me twice since then."

Thomas clenches his hand, crumpling his napkin.

"But I thankfully remain unscathed," I add quickly. "I've fallen into the company of a family that makes it their duty to slay monsters- "

"Then where were they when I needed help?!" Thomas demands, shedding all remains of courtesy and normalcy. "Where were they when I faced the wolf alone?!"

"Amos was tracking it."

Thomas stands quickly, knocking his chair over and throwing his fork at the ground. He scowls at it for a moment before frowning and picking it back up. Then he turns his back to me.

"Thomas?" I whisper.

"Where were they," he asks, still not facing me, "when it did *this* to me?" Thomas pulls his sleeve down, revealing his shoulder- and the infected bite mark on it. "I'm a monster, Jane. That's why I had to leave. And I thought you were safe from the wolf, or I would have hunted him down and killed him more effectively." He turns around, revealing the tears in his eyes. "I'm sorry, Jane. I've failed. I couldn't kill the beast and now I *am* the beast."

I swallow hard as logic says 'I told you so' as it forces me to accept the reality I dared to hope wasn't real. "Thomas, you are neither a monster nor a beast. You're my brother."

"I'll have to hunt down the wolf again," Thomas continues like he hasn't heard me. "I'll have to miss my ship unless I can kill the thing before tomorrow."

I lick my lips which are suddenly very dry. "Where were you going?"

"Scotland."

"Why?"

"To find our mother."

It should have surprised me to learn that my brother is a werewolf, but it didn't. It should have surprised me to see my brother throw his fork on the floor or even that he bothered to pick it back up, but no. What surprises me is hearing the word 'mother' attached to a tangible location. "Is she there? Can she help you? How do you know of these things?"

"Father told me when he told me about the wolf," Thomas answers quietly. "And I don't know if she's there this very moment, but that's her base of operations. As for help, she's my best chance."

"Does that chance have something to do with her mysterious time-consuming job?"

"Yeah, about that..." Thomas rubs the back of his neck. "Father told me of her job, and I don't blame you if you don't believe me..."

"Thomas, I'm talking to a werewolf; I'll believe you."

"Do you really have to go calling names?"

"You were calling names first... We're straying from the subject."

"Right; well, Mother is apparently a faerie godmother." Thomas's face is dead serious.

I can't tell if this surprises me or not- I'm still getting over the whole Scotland thing- so I just nod. "And you believe she can cure you?"

"I hope she can, but first I have to slay the wolf so you'll be safe while I'm gone."

"No," I counter. "Just take me with you. Then we can both get cured." And the wolf won't have to die.

Wait; why would I want that?

I glance down at my formerly sore side and I can't help but wonder what might happen to me if the wolf dies when I already feel his pain; would possibly miss his voice-

Wait; did I just *think* that?

"Jane, the scar really isn't that noticeable," Thomas assures.

"It's not that, Thomas." I clear my throat. "The scar... it links my mind to the wolf's. We're connected."

Thomas frowns. "What do you mean?"

"I can feel his emotions, see through his eyes, and even talk to him across distances."

"Then killing it is still the solution," Thomas says. "Unless... would it kill you too?"

I cringe at the thought. "I- I don' t know.... But you can't miss the ship. If you take me with you, you can protect me."

"Or accidentally kill you myself."

"That would never happen."

"But if I go wolf-"

"Don't you still control your own actions?"

He nods slowly. "Yes... But it's harder. So much harder."

"Thomas, the wolf may have bitten you, but he spared your life- because I asked him, and he listened. If the wolf could do that, then you could too. Besides, I want to be with you in your time of need."

"I wouldn't have much trouble convincing the captain..." He begins before shaking his head. "No; neither of us is going on that ship. I'm killing the wolf and taking the next ship- alone. The wolf may still be injured, and I'm young, so it should be an easy enough fight. As long as I kill him before your birthday, you'll be safe."

I shake my head sadly. "My birthday is no longer the deadline; he's already tried to make me turn several times. If you were to leave me while you hunt the wolf, I'd be vulnerable. If we were on the ship together, though, you could protect me while I took care of you, away from the wolf and on our way to Mother for the cure of both our ailments. You have to listen to me."

Thomas rubs his chin thoughtfully. "Let's say we *do* leave the wolf behind, I *am* able to control my lycanthropy, and we *do* find Mother, who *is* able to cure us. What of Father? Is he already..."

"He was alive last I saw him," I assure. "And recovering at that. He is somewhere safe- from werewolves especially."

Thomas nods slowly. "I will... consider your plan."

I smile.

Suddenly, someone knocks on the shack so hard, I half expect it to come tumbling down.

"Stay here," Thomas orders, cautiously opening the door a crack.

"Excuse me," a familiar voice says on the other side.

"Have you seen a young lady come through here? She looks- a little like a female you, actually."

"I'm sorry," Thomas answers, shutting the door.

"Wait a moment-" the person says. Then he begins pushing his way in.

Thomas scowls, but I quickly hurry over before anything regrettable can happen. Then I remember the manners I was never actually taught. "Thomas, meet Amos- and, oh, Debra too."

~~~

"It's wonderful that you've found your brother," Amos tells me as he studies Thomas from across the table.

"Yes," I agree, trying to distract his study with my pacing, but to no avail. "And it's wonderful that you're recovered."

"Quite." He still doesn't take his eyes off Thomas.

"I should probably return your hat," I add, putting it in between Amos and Thomas. "Thank you for allowing me to borrow it."

Amos just puts the hat back on his head without moving his gaze from Thomas.

I suppress a groan and glance over to where Debra is sitting on the bed even though I know she won't be able to help me, let alone want to.

"When you met the wolf, were you injured in any way, Thomas?" Amos asks.

"I've taken care of that question already," I answer hurriedly. "The true question here is, how did you find me again? And don't say rumors, because I wore my hair up and under a hat this time."

Amos finally tears his gaze from Thomas to me. "My sword is made of silver. As you may know, silver can slay vampires and werewolves. What you probably don't know is that it can track them too. Because of the lycanthropy in your blood, you are vaguely traceable with my sword."

I frown. Did he know I was following him that day? I can't believe I was so ignorant of such an important fact- and probably made a huge fool of myself.

"Strangely enough," Amos adds casually, "this company is giving off a stronger signal than just Jane's usual lycanthropy."

I frown deeper. "Perhaps my bond with the wolf grows stronger with time."

Amos glances warily at Thomas again. "Perhaps."

"Speaking of werewolves," Debra says, finally coming to my aid, though probably unintentionally. "The wolf that attacked us the other night is obviously not dead as Jane is still connected with it, and night is falling. Amos, we need to seek shelter- "

"Why not stay here for the night?" Thomas asks hospitably. "It isn't much, I know, but it's the least I can do for you after you protected my sister for so long."

I try to motion to my brother to take back his words, but Amos nods. "Thank you. That would be just splendid, old sport."

I suppress another groan. The four of us are like the four winds, each trying to blow in a separate direction, and between all our stubbornness, we are in for a stormy night. But I *will* weather the storm. All I have to do is keep Amos and Debra from learning about Thomas, and keep Thomas from deciding that Amos can take better care of me than he can- that's all.

This is going to be some storm.

Chapter Fifteen
In which a nightmare becomes reality and reality becomes a nightmare

"So," Debra begins, no doubt noticing the very thing I've been wondering about, "where are we all going to sleep?"

And so, that's how Amos ends up sprawled out on the table, with Thomas back in the chairs, and Debra and me both trying to use the same tiny bed.

"Why on earth are you staying in *this* hut, Thomas?" I mutter. Sure, he probably had no money on him when he came here, but that's no excuse for such squalor.

"Because this is the only one they'd actually pay *me* to stay in," Thomas answers. "I know- if I stay here much longer, I'll have to ask for an increase in rent."

"*Shh*," Debra mutters, taking more of my side of the bed than I am.

"It's a good thing you're not planning on staying here much longer, Thomas," I hint.

"Why?" Amos asks. "Where are you going?"

"I have to go hunt the wolf hunting my sister," Thomas answers.

I bite my lip; he took that the wrong way. "No you're not."

"No you're not," Amos agrees. "That's my job."

Uh-oh; dangerous territory. "Uh, yeah; Amos can take care of it while you and I go our separate ways together, Thomas."

"Actually, you still need to come back to my parents' home for your anger management skills, Miss," Amos counters.

"I'm trying to sleep here, people," Debra snaps.

"Somebody else needs anger management," I mutter.

Debra elbows me in the back.

"He's right, Jane," Thomas agrees. "You need anger management."

No, I need a complete cure. "But I need to be with you."

"And what about Father?" he points out.

"How about we talk about this in the morning?" Debra asks.

For once I agree with her- maybe by then I can come up with a plan.

"Or we can talk about this *now*," Thomas growls slightly.

"Maybe you could use anger management too, Thomas," Amos says. "Are you sure the wolf didn't scratch you or anything, old sport?"

Uh-oh; dangerous territory in a different way.

"I assure you that he didn't scratch me," Thomas answers.

"It's true," I agree. "Now can we go to sleep?"

This time, the boys listen. Debra, however, doesn't seem to like my idea of getting some sleep- at least for *my* getting some sleep- because she succeeds in conquering the rest of the bed, leaving me to somehow manage to find some sleep on the hard floor of the hut.

~~~

Come to me, my pet. Come to me, captor of my heart,

beloved of my soul.

Suddenly, something wet lapping at my ankles. I open my eyes and find myself outside, standing in the shallows of the bay, in the darkness of either late night or early dawn.

Huh?

Come to me, my pet. And stay in the water, so your brother cannot track your scent.

Suddenly, I realize what must have happened: I sleepwalked- followed the wolf's commands in my sleep. How far have I come? And how close to the wolf?

Heart thumping wildly, I glance around just as wildly, searching for the shack. Finally, I spot it just within viewing distance. I focus my eyes on the shack and *run*.

Wrong way, my pet.

I keep running, refusing to wonder if *I* am within *his* view.

Don't make me chase you.

I scream for the sheer terror of it all, but I don't dare slow my pace; don't dare look back.

The shack door bursts open and Amos, Debra, and Thomas hurry out. "Jane?!"

I'm too breathless to call out to them, so I keep running, desperately hoping that they'll see me.

And all too aware that something is chasing me.

That something is right behind me.

Suddenly, I trip, and a wolf leaps over me. Then it skids to a stop and whips around. I find myself looking up at the wolf that had marked me as a child, that's plagued my dreams, and that hurt Amos that fateful night.

You are mine.

Suddenly, it goes flying sideways. Another werewolf with auburn fur instead black is on it, biting and clawing at it.

Amos hurries over to me. "Jane?"

"I'm not bitten," I assure shakily.

He nods and hurries over to the two wrestling wolves. One of whom I have no doubt is my brother.

Debra takes Amos' place by my side. "Jane?"

I ignore her and tilt my head to get a better view of the battle. The wolves are both still wrestling like ferocious animals. Amos holds his sword above them, and I can't help but wonder if he cares which wolf his sword punctures.

He doesn't.

Resolutely, I stand up again and then dive at Amos, knocking us both to the side, just like Thomas did to the wolf.

"Jane!" Amos cries.

"I won't let you hurt my brother!" I answer.

"I wasn't- "

"He's not something I can risk."

"So you'll let the wolf kill him instead? What are you thinking?"

I reach for my dagger but then shake my head; it won't be enough. Instead I snatch up Amos' fallen sword, sending a shiver down my spine. What am I thinking? Something worthy of praise, I hope.

Hurrying over to the brawling wolves, I raise my sword over the pair, waiting for my chance. A tear slides down my face in anticipation of the pain; the loss.

No, this monster is a danger to both my family and my

friends. It must die, even if I die with it.

I bring the sword down on the black wolf, and it howls with pain. I howl with it.

The black wolf tosses my brother off of itself and staggers away. Then it breaks into a run.

And I almost think I see it shrink back into a man in the distance, but the morning mist conceals him.

Pain. Shock. Anger. Sorrow. Pain. Heartbreak.

I fall to my knees. The wolf is not dead; I have merely wounded it. It will take much more effort to succeed in killing the monster.

But, painful as it was, I *have* won this particular battle.

Yet he's still out there, and he still wants me. And not just my mind either. Now I know, he wants all of me- starting with my heart.

My brother, the wolf, stands up and shakes himself. I reach out and touch a sore. Thomas shudders again, but he doesn't attack me.

"My sword please, Miss," Amos says behind me.

I glance between him and Thomas. Thomas and I come to a silent agreement.

"Good-bye," I say. Then I hand Amos his sword before jumping onto Thomas's back. Together, we run off, away from menacing werewolves and confused werewolf hunters, focused on Scotland and the cure we hope to find there.

Acknowledgments:

The imagination of an author is a scary (at least the minds of horror and romance authors are) and convoluted (this is pretty much true for all of us, I think), and it takes a lot of work to go from a great idea to a great book. Here are some of the people who helped along the way. The Poetry Foundation for their copies of the poems reprinted in this series- and, of course, the poets themselves. Also, *http://www.citrus.k12.fl.us/staffdev/Social%20Studies/PDF/Slang%20of%20the%201920s.pdf* for some 1920s slang tips. Clean Reads Publishing, who even though they didn't take it, still saved my manuscript when I lost my own copy. The Smiths for being just so plain nice. Stefanidi Marina for these gorgeous covers. The other people around me who give me ideas just by living out their day-to-day lives. And, of course, my family: my brothers, especially Caleb, who was one of the first to read this book (if not *the* first, considering how long ago it was); my grandma, who also proofread it (and I have the pages of studiously copied notes to prove it); my sister, for actually liking it; my mother, for helping in various little ways even if she won't read it until it's published; and my father, who helped as always. And above all, to my Lord Jesus Christ- author of my story Who lets me play with a few stories of my own.

ABOUT THE AUTHOR

Jes Drew, like most teenage girls, was swept away by the Twilight saga, but even though she was totally team Edward, she found herself strangely fascinated by werewolves. One bran picture later, and Jane was born- and wouldn't be ignored, so the rest of her story was birthed. Jes lives with her mom, dad, younger sister, four (yes, four) younger brothers, a German shepherd named Rylie and a teddy bear puppy named Zoey. She is the author of The Ninja and Hunter. Besides writing, Jes also enjoys drawing, reading, working, and daydreaming. You can contact her at-http://pausefortales.blogspot.com

Disclaimer:

The author does not actually believe that Baptist churches are any less sacred than other churches. She just likes to poke fun at her brothers and sisters in Christ every now and then. It's normal. If you have siblings, you'll understand.

Another Disclaimer:

Also, just because the author had a Catholic priest in her story does not mean that she, herself, is one of them papists. More teasing siblings. She is actually nondenominational, so she only has to worry about being teased about being a Christian.

Also Available (thankfully):

The Ninja and Hunter trilogy:
   Book one: *The Time I Saved the Day*
   Book two: *The Time I Saved a Damsel in Distress*
   Book three: *The Time I Saved the World*

Coming Soon (Lord willing):

The Howling Twenties trilogy continued:
   Book two: *Wolf Curse*
   Book three: *Wolf Cure*

The Kristian Clark saga:
   Book one: *Kristian Clark and Holy Heist*

The Castaways trilogy:
   Book one: *Castaways*
   Book two: *Fugitives*
   Book three: *Targets*

You may also enjoy Nicki Chapelway's Books:

My Time in Amar
> Book One: *A Week of Werewolves, Faeries, and Fancy Dresses*
> Book Two: *A Time of Trepidation, Pirates, and Lost Princesses* (Coming Soon)

Made in the USA
Lexington, KY
18 January 2018